SMALL DISPLAYS OF
CHAOS

 bitlit

A **free** eBook edition is available
with the purchase of this print book.

SMALL DISPLAYS OF
CHAOS

BREANNA FISCHER

Edited by Kathy Stinson
Book designed by Jamie Olson
Typeset by Susan Buck
Printed and bound in Canada

Library and Archives Canada Cataloguing in Publication

Fischer, Breanna, author
        Small displays of chaos / Breanna Fischer.

Issued in print and electronic formats.
ISBN 978-1-55050-661-7 (paperback).--ISBN 978-1-55050-662-4 (pdf).--
ISBN 978-1-55050-663-1 (html).--ISBN 978-1-55050-664-8 (html)

        I. Title.

PS8611.I775S63 2016   jC813'.6   C2015-908771-6
                                                   C2015-908772-4

Library of Congress Control Number   9781550506617

COTEAU
BOOKS

2517 Victoria Avenue
Regina, Saskatchewan
Canada S4P 0T2
www.coteaubooks.com

Available in Canada from:
Publishers Group Canada
2440 Viking Way
Richmond, British Columbia
Canada V6V 1N2

Available in the US from:
Orca Book Publishers
www.orcabook.com
1-800-210-5277

10 9 8 7 6 5 4 3 2 1

Coteau Books gratefully acknowledges the financial support of its publishing program by: the Saskatchewan Arts Board, The Canada Council for the Arts, the Government of Saskatchewan through Creative Saskatchewan, the City of Regina. We further acknowledge the [financial] support of the Government of Canada. Nous reconnaissons l'appui [financier] du gouvernement du Canada.

For my mom and dad,
for always giving me a safe place to come home to.

chapter one

September

RAYANNE TIMKO WAS CERTAIN that she could handle the first
week back at school. The fact that she was a senior now
had no sentimental effect on her; kids at school still joined
the same teams, skipped the same classes, and smoked by
the same stairwell. As far as she was concerned, nothing
had changed.

Except for *this*.

This being the wooden door marked *Tracy Boyer,
School Counsellor*. She'd never stepped foot in the office
in her life, not even to discuss switching her classes or to
begin planning for university. Now, the door was an im-
posing façade, staring her down from across the hall of the
Student Services Office. She fidgeted in the uncomfortable
waiting room chair.

Rayanne's goal in high school was similar to a criminal's
in a heist: get in, get out, and be seen by no one. Gaining
the attention of a Guidance Counsellor at all was the first

chink in that plan. Four years into the game. And it had been going so *well*.

Ms Boyer poked her head out of the door. She had tanned skin and arching, dark eyebrows. Her eyes were kind though.

Rayanne catalogued this as an imminent threat.

"Rayanne?"

She gave a short nod. Ms Boyer smiled and leaned her head into her office, indicating Rayanne should come in.

She did, grabbing last year's backpack by its worn handle. The first day of school and it was already heavy, though the day's lectures had leaked out of her head by now. She couldn't remember what her homework was supposed to be about or for. Hopefully she had written it down.

The chair facing the desk in Ms Boyer's small, dimly lit office looked soft and comforting. Rayanne hesitated before sitting and nestling her backpack beside her leg.

Aside from her homework, the bag held a well-used purple spiral notebook, which was Rayanne's entire life.

"It's nice to meet you. Officially." Ms Boyer smiled, sitting at the chair behind her desk. Rayanne read the message under the words: they hadn't met unofficially, either, unless you counted Ms Boyer conspiring with Rayanne's mother, Hannah, as an appropriate introduction. Which Rayanne didn't.

Still, she smiled politely.

"You're nervous," Ms Boyer stated intuitively, but gently, as she cleared some papers and a stained to-go coffee cup from her desk. Rayanne gave her signature gesture: one shoulder lifted in a half-shrug.

"I've never done this before."

"Done what?" Placing a clean piece of paper and a pen

on her desk, Ms Boyer settled down now, leaning back a little and looking at Ray with kind interest. Rayanne shifted.

"Counselling."

"We don't have to call it anything. We're just talking."

Rayanne pressed her lips shut. A few moments of silence passed. Ms Boyer clicked her pen.

"Your mom thought this would be a good idea. You don't agree?"

Again, Rayanne shrugged. "I don't know."

Another beat of silence. Ms Boyer switched tactics. "You said yourself you've never been to counselling before. Why do you think that may be changing now?"

Rayanne studied her hands. This was the first of a standing appointment she had with the counsellor every week, but Ray didn't know to what end. She knew what her parents suspected, but she could never say as much out loud.

"Help me out here, Ray," Ms Boyer said. "I just want to get to know you."

"No you don't," Ray finally replied in clipped syllables. "People don't ask those questions when they want to get to know someone. They ask questions like…what movies do you like, or what music are you into?"

"Okay." Ms Boyer went along easily. "What kind of movies do you like?"

Rayanne fell quiet again. She glared at Ms Boyer steadily.

Ms Boyer pretended to look hurt. "Come on, Ray. I'm playing by your rules, here."

Rayanne shifted her glare to the framed picture of Buffy St. Marie on the wall. "Dramas."

Ms Boyer nodded. "Romantic dramas?"

Rayanne scrunched her nose. "No. Like – indie dramas, I guess. Movies about real things and real people, with preferably bittersweet endings."

This seemed to amuse Ms Boyer – her lip quirked up in the corner. A few seconds of silence passed again.

"So asking a person about their favourite things – that's the way you get to know them?" she asked, not unkindly. Rayanne wasn't sure how to answer.

"I guess."

Ms Boyer gave a slow nod. "What's your favourite season?"

Rayanne hesitated. "Summer."

"Favourite…Christmas song?"

"O Holy Night."

"Favourite food?"

Now, Rayanne's lips sealed shut.

Rayanne's favourite food was homemade potato and onion perogies. No cheese, because she felt even that deliciously sinful food would muddy the purity that is potato wrapped in dough. She didn't care if they were fried or boiled, just that they were swimming in butter, speckled with fresh pepper, and made by either her mother or her Baba.

"I don't have one," she said, even as her mouth watered. She thought of helping her mom make homemade perogies at Thanksgiving; dipping her fingers in warm water to seal the dough; Hannah reminding her to try and keep the flour off her clothes, please.

"You don't have a favourite food?" Ms Boyer's eyebrows lifted in surprise. Ray shook her head.

"Nope."

"What about when you were a kid?"

"I can't remember."

Ms Boyer frowned, but only subtly. "When I was a child, my favourite food was birthday cake. The vanilla kind, with rainbow sprinkles. Now, it's my husband's French Onion Soup."

Rayanne just nodded. She wasn't sure what she was supposed to say; mostly, she was focusing on not letting her stomach growl.

Ms Boyer watched her for a moment.

"I have a theory," Ms Boyer went on softly, "that our favourite foods change over time, not with our taste buds, but with our lives. Because food tastes like different places and times. Different memories."

Rayanne focused on the hem of her shirtsleeves. She could hear Ms Boyer's words, but she couldn't feel them – as if they were black flies throwing themselves against a pane of glass, while Rayanne watched from the other side.

"Anyway…" Ms Boyer shifted a little and dropped her gaze, as if sensing her subject was shutting down. "It's interesting to think about."

Rayanne didn't reply.

When her session was over, Rayanne walked out with "homework" which involved cataloging her favourite things. And while Ms Boyer said it was so she could know Rayanne better, Rayanne suspected it was also an effort to uncover somebody she had been, before she'd become somebody who goes to weekly counselling at all.

She understood that Ms Boyer and her parents were trying to prevent "the problem" from tail-spinning any more, but she also knew that most of what they were attempting to prevent had already come to pass.

chapter two

TWO YEARS AGO, Rayanne found this hidden life: a secret that was hers and no one else's.

Her tenth grade uniform was the same as everybody else's. That was the whole point. Still, Rayanne couldn't stop staring at how the clothes fit the other girls in her class. Somehow, the thick fabric and too-large sizes didn't look awkward on them. Most of the girls had the elastics of their shorts rolled, to make them shorter. Their dark-blue shirts bunched around slim but toned arms.

They were supposed to be stretching before playing badminton, but most of the girls were just talking. Rayanne looked down at her own legs. Her skin was pale after a summer of working inside. She could see faint blue veins and tiny, translucent blond hairs. She must have forgotten to shave that morning.

Swallowing around self-consciousness, Rayanne pulled at her shorts again.

She was a good student. Aside from Amy, the oldest of her sisters, Rayanne had the best grades in the family. English was her best subject by far, though she had to study extra hard for all sciences. She'd made honour roll in her freshmen year.

Phys Ed was always a different story. She counted herself lucky her other grades made up for it.

The Phys Ed teacher, Mrs. Shears, appeared from the gym offices with a stack of papers in her hand. Rayanne's heart leapt hopefully when she started passing them around.

"All right, girls," she called, her voice echoing around the gymnasium's rafters. "It's sophomore year. That means take-home assignments are now a part of our curriculum."

A few of the girls groaned. Rayanne took her paper eagerly and read it over.

The premise of the assignment was simple: pick a "fitness goal" to reach by the end of the term, and journal about it. Rayanne picked the same goal as the majority of her class: eat healthier, exercise more.

Health and fitness had never really been on Rayanne's radar before. Aside from her mother telling her to finish her food, and not to eat dessert first, she didn't give either a second thought.

But the act of writing and tallying her daily food and activities quickly became a comfortable ritual. Adding and subtracting the numbers had a certain satisfaction to it, especially when they tallied in her favour.

Each time she attended one of her mother's fitness classes, or switched out full-fat dressing for the "lite" option, it was with the thought of how nicely those equations would work out. And she had no inkling that this train of thought was addictive at all.

The first month, she lost seven pounds.

Her favourite activity was running. At the root of it, maybe the adrenaline that pumped in her heart was born of memories of freeze-tag in the park and sprinting to some made-up Home Free. But the music on her "run" playlist went from energetic to angry.

Smarter, faster, stronger. It became a mantra to her, and it soon became clear to Rayanne that if she wanted to be faster, she should be thinner. Smaller people were more aerodynamic; the less weight she carried around, the faster she'd be.

If she wanted to be stronger, she should be thinner. Thin is a sign of the strong: strong enough to diligently strip away the fat, the extra parts of yourself to find who you really are, hiding beneath.

And of course, receiving a high grade in Phys Ed would boost her honour roll grade to *distinction* status. She was smart enough to make those daily numbers work in her favour; for once *gym* would work in her favour.

Smarter, faster, stronger. It was Rayanne's trinity.

At the very end of her assignment, Rayanne ran four kilometers every other day, had completely cut out sugars and "bad" carbs, and had an intricate understanding of "good" and "bad" fats.

Her grade was one of the highest in the class. But while the rest of the girls moved on to a new assignment, the last one already forgotten, Rayanne felt a sense of loss – a distant sort of *what now* feeling.

Two weeks passed after the assignment, and Rayanne missed her journal with an ache that distracted her at each mealtime.

She bought a new one.

Each morning, Rayanne would look in the bathroom's

full-length mirror. She could see baby fat still clinging to her legs and stomach, waiting to convert to grown-up fat that would never go away.

Each night, she took inventory. The edges of her shoulders, ribs pressing beneath skin: one, two, three. There was fat lining her stomach and rolls around her sides. Then sharp hipbones, so envied that she couldn't help but be proud of them.

Her thighs, however, bothered her.

She thought of all the extra parts of her body: skin clinging to fat, fat clinging to muscle, and knew that her bones, and the person who she wanted to be, were hiding somewhere underneath.

chapter three

MS BOYER'S APPOINTMENT took up the last class period of the day. Afterward, Rayanne found Carina waiting by their locker. The school had assigned the sisters separate ones, just like every year, but as always they gravitated toward one another.

Rayanne was grateful for the fact that she and Carina weren't identical. It allowed her the safe illusion of independence. While Rayanne's dark hair was long and thin, Carina's spilled over her shoulders in thick waves. Ray had a sharper chin, a more angular nose, and dark brown eyes. Carina's heart-shaped face held soft features, punctuated by a sharp hazel gaze.

Carina obsessively straightened the magnet mirror on the back of the locker door. Charmayne and Madison, two of their group of five, talked animatedly about their elective Physical Education class, which Rayanne had been fast to pass on.

Madison was a spunky, loud-mouthed kid with blond hair and too many freckles. Char was a taller girl with warm brown eyes and skin to match. Her long, black hair always started the day loose around her shoulders, before Char trained it back into a braid sometime around noon.

Leaning between the pair and Carina, was Kayla: the fifth of their Group of Five, and Carina's best friend (aside from Rayanne).

"Here she is." Kayla teased as Ray approached, "the child prodigy. How was tutoring?"

Rayanne's cheeks burned, and she avoided Carina's gaze as she grabbed her jacket from inside the locker. Only a week into September, and already the wind brought goose bumps to Rayanne's skin.

"About as fun as tutoring can be," she said shortly, hoping to communicate that she didn't want to talk about it.

She knew Kayla wouldn't pick up on the hint, but Carina did. She was the only one who knew that Rayanne wasn't tutoring a freshman, like she'd told their friends.

"How was geek gym?" Carina asked Madison and Charmayne.

"Dude, it was *awesome*." Madison slammed her locker door shut and clicked the lock back in place. "Char almost tipped our kayak over. It was hilarious."

"That was your fault!" Char shot back, closing her own locker. Ray felt a laugh bubbling past her lips, but it was more reflex than real emotion. The more she laughed, the less worried questions her friends asked.

The girls finished at their lockers and began walking down the halls. Ray could see the faces of familiar people as they passed, calling to one another. The girls moved through the riot of activity easily, because they were seniors and this was all routine by now.

Another routine of Rayanne's, since the ninth grade, was to scan the halls for a last glimpse of green eyes and a dark hoodie. But on the first Thursday of her senior year, she kept her eyes trained to the movement of her friends' sneakers, certain those parting glances weren't something she deserved.

SATURDAY MORNING was for sleeping in.

Rayanne woke up at eight.

At eight-fifteen, she weighed herself in the bathroom she shared with Carina to find that she was 104 pounds. Exactly one pound less than the day before.

At eight-twenty, she padded up the carpet stairs to the floor above.

The house was dead quiet that morning. Rayanne loved it. She loved the way she could hear the heating hum to life – could witness the quiet, cool morning outside the windows that belonged only to the birds.

She made a cup of coffee: black. She toasted a single slice of brown bread, which she spread with minimal low-fat margarine and even less peanut butter.

Rayanne didn't bother with minute measurements. As long as she was eating her own food, at the proper time and at her own pace, then everything was good. *There's nothing wrong, this is fine, everything's fine.*

After her toast, she ate a fat-free yogurt cup. Then she washed her dishes and put them back, and swept the crumbs off the counter. When she grabbed her coffee cup off the counter (still steaming), Ray could idly register the fuel in her stomach and the energy slowly seeping into her bones.

She retreated downstairs before anyone else had made

a sound. If it weren't for the pot of coffee already waiting, there would've been no sign she had been up at all.

RAYANNE HAD MORE relatives than she could count, and over half of them were Ukrainian. It seemed random for a city like Saskatoon, Saskatchewan, but she'd never questioned it. She grew up seeing Ukrainian Orthodox churches scattered around the city, and Hannah helped them make pysanky and braided bread each Easter.

Every once in a while, the girls would get to go to a Ukrainian wedding. Rayanne had loved them because they were like a carnival of lights, music, and colour.

When her cousin Tatiana – three years her senior – got engaged to an engineering student with a trust fund, she chose Rayanne and her sisters, along with a handful of other cousins, to be in her bridal party.

The last time Rayanne had actually talked with Tatiana, the girls were in grade school. Tatiana's favourite TV show then was *Rugrats* and she was always bragging about the trampoline in her backyard. Rayanne loved Raffi and habitually ate only the icing off of cupcakes.

She doubted they had much in common now.

Luckily, the bride and her frenzied entourage couldn't be present at that Saturday morning's particular dress fitting. It was only Jordie, Amy, Carina and Ray, along with their mother at a bridal store that sat across from the Midtown Plaza.

"I still don't understand why *we're* bridesmaids." Jordie spoke Rayanne's sentiments out loud, but with confusion instead of distaste. As it was, the youngest Timko girl looked around at the dresses with hungry eyes. Her bleached blond hair didn't match ninety percent of the fabrics.

13

Their mom shrugged, "Some brides like big weddings." She wore her usual outfit of comfortable Lulu's and a knit sweater. Her dark, curly hair was, as always, pulled back into an exploding ponytail.

"Still," Jordie pressed. "how many bridesmaids does Tatiana have?"

Rayanne counted in her head. "Twelve, including us."

"Jesus Christ." Carina sighed and sat down on the changeroom couch. Rayanne sat beside her.

"Language, Carrie," Hannah said calmly.

The changeroom curtain flashed open, and Amy stepped out from behind it. She was the same height as Rayanne, despite being four years older. Her light brown hair had been converted to dreadlocks years ago, though she was considering shaving them off for the wedding. The silver piercings in her eyebrow, nose and lip glinted beneath the changeroom lights, and her various tattoos were in full view.

She was wearing Tatiana's final choice of a bridesmaid dress: a little strapless number in a dark, deep burgundy. It reminded Rayanne of the merlot her mom drank when the weather got cold.

The saleslady appeared around the corner and encouraged Amy to step up on a wooden pedestal in front of a three-paned mirror. Rayanne squirmed.

"The colour goes perfectly with her complexion, I must say," the saleslady said, reaching out and tugging a little at the fabric of the dress. Amy stiffened. "And the fabric is a *gorgeous* chiffon. Miss Boyko made a lovely choice."

Hannah hummed. "I agree."

She walked up to Amy and began playing with the fabric in places. Rayanne watched Amy's jaw bunch, but Amy must have swallowed down any sass she felt bubbling to the surface because she stayed quiet.

The saleslady moved around Amy, feeling the width of her ribs and hips. Rayanne swallowed forcefully and closed her eyes.

When she opened them, Rayanne saw Edie leaning delicately against the leather couches. Edie was different from Rayanne in one key aspect: Edie was about twenty pounds lighter.

She regarded Rayanne with shrewd eyes.

Rayanne reassured herself for the hundredth time that, technically, Edie wasn't an imaginary friend. She knew that Edie wasn't real.

Rayanne's hands shook when she saw her, but that wasn't anything new. She'd never had steady hands.

Rayanne was always thinking in terms of a past and present self, and she wondered if the future Rayanne would be someone who had steady hands, or if things like confidence and bravery were things you had to be born with.

Edie glared at Amy' s dress, even though it was obvious why she had shown up in the first place. Rayanne's eyes darted to Amy's slim-fitting dress, the flimsy change-room curtains, and the three-paned mirror.

She looked at Edie with wide eyes. *I hate this.*

When Ray closed her eyes, Edie's cold, small hand slid into hers and Ray felt her frosty breath against her ear.

I know.

chapter four

EARLY MONDAY MORNING, Rayanne stepped onto the cold steel of her bathroom scale. The house was quiet but for the sound of Rayanne holding her breath as the numbers climbed up, up.

They ticked past 90, slowed at 96. Settled on 100.

Edie regarded her in the bathroom mirror. She never showed up after a weigh-in these days – not when the scale showed a number like 100.

It had been Rayanne's goal weight for years.

Ninety, she whispered.

Rayanne accepted this new goal weight as if she'd been expecting it from the very beginning. In the back of her mind, she had the dim suspicion that Edie would never be satisfied. But Rayanne kept holding on to the hope that something would happen; something would come along and erase Edie from her life forever, before she followed Edie's never-ending orders into the ground.

Later, she sat in her fifth period world religions class scribbling the number 90 in her journal.

The next fitting was in two weeks, and Rayanne was frantic. Every time she closed her eyes, she swore she could feel wrinkled hands pulling ribbons tighter around her ribs. She had to remind herself she was still able to breathe.

Suddenly, Rayanne was aware that she was digging her fingernails into her wrist. She immediately stopped, placing her hands on top of her desk instead and trying to tune back in to Mrs. Davie's lecture.

"Now that we have some time…" The teacher glanced at the clock. There were twenty minutes left until the bell. "…I'll pass out the guidelines for this year's community service requirements."

As expected, the class collectively groaned.

Last year, the juniors were required to put in fifteen hours of community service. As seniors, it was twenty. The idea, Rayanne was told, was to teach them responsibility and (she supposed) compassion before releasing them into the world. Rayanne logged her hours with Carina at a daycare in the Y, colouring with kids while their parents attended one of the programs. All in all, not a bad way to spend four weekends out of the year.

This year, Rayanne knew what she wanted to do with her volunteer hours. It's what she'd wanted to do from the get-go, but her mother hadn't allowed it.

Something told Ray she might able to talk her into it, this year. Because it had been months since Rayanne had wanted to do *anything*, so how could Hannah rightfully stop her now?

"You'll find a list of appropriate organizations and foundations on the second page." Mrs. Davie explained.

She passed stapled pieces of paper out to the class, while some of the students took advantage of her distraction to text under their desks. "I'll remind you that babysitting for money, or collecting bottles for profit, does not constitute community service."

A kid at the front raised his hand. A few students chuckled apprehensively. Ray always chose the seats by the windows, because it made her feel less trapped.

Mrs. Davie pursed her lips. "Jason?" Her voice was deadpan. Ray snickered.

"What about providing for the sick?"

"Selling marijuana to cancer patients does not count, Jason. We talked about this." Mrs. Davie looked around as the class laughed. "Anyone else?"

As a few other hands went up, to ask actual questions, Rayanne let her gaze wander to the boy a few desks ahead of her.

Josh Reid sat with his chin resting on his folded arms, head angled slightly toward the window. Ray wondered if his green eyes were looking outside, if he was paying attention to what Mrs. Davie was saying at all. He wore his usual dark hoodie, dirty jeans, and Converse sneakers. A snapback hat lay in his lap, as they weren't permitted to wear them in class. Classic Boy Clothes.

Rayanne didn't know why she did this: why she'd catalogue everything about him, and then dutifully walk out the door and down the hall, never glancing back.

Edie perched on the windowsill beside Rayanne.

You know why, she said. And Rayanne did. Boys were distracting, and more than that, for people *not like her*.

Rayanne took the handout Mrs. Davie gave her, focusing on the printed words instead of the blond-brown hair ahead of her.

When the bell rang, Rayanne bolted. She had just made it into the hall when a voice called her.

She turned back to see Josh walking up to her, shrugging a little self-consciously around the crowds of kids filtering into the halls. The noise rose to the ceiling, but Rayanne could still hear her heart beating.

"Hey," she said quietly, just trying the word, like a sip of hot coffee. It burned.

Josh stopped in front of her. Close enough to smell the laundry detergent on his clothes, and some typical boy scent like Adidas body spray.

"How've you been?" he asked.

Horrible. Lonely. Cold. "Okay, I guess. You?"

Josh rubbed the back of his neck. "Same."

Ray just nodded. There was a beat of silence.

"So." Josh actually looked at her, instead of at her shoes. "I know we sort of drifted apart. Or whatever. But I kinda miss hanging out with you."

Shame washed over Rayanne, but she answered, "Me too."

ON THE TWINS' BIRTHDAY the winter before, Kayla's house was packed to the walls. A demolished birthday cake sat on the table: yellow-white layers with thick white frosting. The sprinkles were green and red – leftovers from Christmas. Their colour had bled into the frosting.

Kayla's old Labrador, Hank, was sitting on the kitchen floor, staring down the cake as if hoping to Jedi-mind-trick it onto the floor. Drool dangled from his lips.

"It'll make you sick," Rayanne told him. He whined.

Rayanne hadn't touched the cake either, because she was off-setting the calories of the booze by not eating at all that day.

Despite her introverted nature, Rayanne didn't mind parties. To her, it sort of made sense – at a packed house party, she could wear the crowd like a cloak.

At some time past midnight, Rayanne had polished off two beer and most of a 26 of spiced rum. She danced in the living room with Madison and Charmayne, feeling the bass move through her fingertips as her body swayed.

Rayanne genuinely liked the way alcohol burned on the way down. She melted into the way it wrapped around her brain, numbing her out and yet helping her float.

She spun in place in the middle of Kayla's living room, lifting her arms to the music and watching lights behind her eyelids. She thought of how, in old stories, jazz girls would always talk about gin and so maybe she was destined for pretty things like they were.

Kayla's bathroom was almost confusingly quiet after the throbbing music in the living room. Rayanne fumbled with the handle on the door, trying to lock it properly and with minimal noise. Blood pounded in her ears, as if to take the music's place.

Ray was aware of her feet stumbling away from the closed bathroom door, the linoleum cold beneath her. She reached a hand out to a wall to steady herself.

Slowly, she slid down the wall until she was sitting on the floor, facing the toilet. The white porcelain blurred in her vision. Her eyes and mouth felt numb. But it was the other parts of her body that she felt too much.

Rayanne's stomach was bloated from the sugar and alcohol – empty calories that she didn't need. She ran her hands across her belly, all too aware of the soft, squishy skin beneath her fingers.

A bang sounded from somewhere outside the door. Voices floated through the walls. Rayanne knew she had to act quickly.

She pulled herself forward onto her knees and clumsily slammed the toilet lid open. Glancing unsteadily at the closed door, Rayanne pulled her hair back with one hand and closed her other in a fist, save for her first two fingers.

When those didn't seem to work, she moved on to a toothbrush she spied on the sink. The faint taste of peppermint touched her tongue as she pressed the handle down her throat.

Vaguely, she registered the sound of someone pounding on the door.

Telling herself they'd assume it was the alcohol, Rayanne pushed harder on the toothbrush. Her stomach muscles contracted, and sick spilled into the toilet bowl. The sound of her gagging bounced off the walls.

Then, the bathroom door flung open, and a blast of noise assaulted the small space before it slammed shut again. She was still gagging, coughing into the back of her hand, but she looked over her shoulder as the lock clicked into place.

Josh stood by the door, frozen only for a moment before crossing the space between them and kneeling down to Rayanne. His jaw was tensed, and his eyes were wide and scared.

"Are you okay? Rayanne." His voice was low and panicked. He looked down at Rayanne, at the dirty toothbrush in her hand. "What's going on?"

Ray dropped her hand behind the toilet, attempting to hide the evidence. With her other hand, she reached out and pushed Josh away.

"I drank too much. Leave me 'lone. Kay?" She tried to make the words firm and authoritative, but they came out slurred and rasped.

She could think of nothing else to say. Her brain felt stalled, broken, and the only thing she could focus on was the way the room had begun to spin.

Rayanne leaned over the toilet and was sick again.

"Jesus," she heard Josh mutter. He sounded more scared than mad. Ray could feel him pull back her hair.

When she was done and sat back on her heels, the floor lurched beneath her. She fell back and smacked her head against the side of the bathtub.

"Fuck, Ray." Josh tried to help her sit up. She groaned in complaint and curled into a ball on the floor.

She closed her eyes. Dimly, she was aware of Josh moving around the bathroom. He flushed the toilet and picked something up off the floor – the toothbrush, Ray assumed – and rinsed it quickly before chucking it in the garbage can.

Ray made a mental note to buy Kayla a new one.

The water ran again, and then Josh gently pulled Ray upright and propped her against the tub. A damp washcloth wiped off her hand, her face; the cool water was soothing.

Her hands shook violently but the nausea had passed. What assaulted her then was a tidal wave of exhaustion.

Josh knelt in front of her again, his eyes serious as he studied her face. Rayanne willed her vision to focus as she looked back.

"Josh," she said quietly, voice barely more than a croak, "can we not talk about this?"

He looked at her a moment, but didn't answer. Instead he pulled her up off the floor and led her out of the bathroom, past throngs of people and downstairs to Kayla's bedroom.

He helped her into the bed before grabbing a trash can and placing it on the ground beside her. The he turned around and walked silently out of the room, closing the door behind him.

chapter five

"YO! REID!" a voice boomed down the hall past the lockers and Josh's friend, Cameron, held one arm in the air. "Ride, or what?"

"Yeah, just..." Josh glanced at Ray. "I'll be right there."

Ray's heart dropped a little, but she was grateful. It would already take at least two hours of non-sleep to properly comb through this interaction, and she didn't think she could take any more.

"Sorry," Josh muttered sullenly, pulling car keys out of his pocket. "I gotta go. But I'll text you, or something?"

For a fraction of a moment, Ray actually let her eyes rest on Josh's. She wasn't sure she liked it.

Still, she found herself saying, "Okay. Cool."

September 22
I feel like some sort of newborn lately. It's strange,

but that's the only way I can describe it. I feel hyper-sensitive to everything – sounds are loud and sharp, textures are extremes of what they would normally be.

I've discovered that I love wrists. Not just wrists, but the inside of them, where the skin seems thin and soft and blue veins trace up your arm to the palm of your hand. It's such a fragile part of a person; you can feel their pulse there, and they seem so breakable.

I can't stop thinking about having sore hands. Not just having them, but the idea of it: everyone has a sore back or sore arms, but to have sore hands? Artists have sore hands; pianists have sore hands. I ache for sore hands, not from disease or arthritis but because you just need to rest or stop or something.

It seems that crying and weeping are different things all together. Weeping is such a pretty word, isn't it? To weep, to be wept over. Poets weep; Jesus wept. I can only ever cry, which seems like a weakness. To weep would be a very brave but human thing to do.

All of this fills my mind, my days: just being human. Red sore hands, fragile breakable bones, breakable heart, soft hair, tired eyes, heavy soul. It makes my heart ache and swell at the same time.

SUPPER THAT NIGHT was vegetable stir-fry. Edie glared at Rayanne's plate as she sat at the dinner table, picking at a piece of broccoli flecked with rice.

Once upon a time, the dinner table at the Timkos' was a riot of noise and activity. As kids, Jordie and Carina were most often fighting for their parents' attention, while Amy threw in her two cents and Rayanne jumped to her defense when it pissed their sisters off.

Amy had moved in with roommates off-campus. Suppers had been growing quieter for the past two years. For once, Jordie had no one to compete with as she rambled on about her volleyball tryouts. Carina stared at her own plate of food, but her eyes were far away.

"What about you girls?" Hannah turned her attention to the twins. "Joining anything? It's your last year."

Carina shrugged and said, "Yearbook. Volleyball. The usual."

Rayanne shook her head. There was nothing at school – no sport team, club, or vocation of any kind – that interested her at all.

"But," she said, "we have to do those community service hours again."

Hannah nodded, and Cal asked, "How many?"

"Twenty," Carina answered, and Cal gave a low whistle.

Before Ray could help herself, she just blurted out, "I want to volunteer at a dog shelter."

Cal fixed his eyes on his plate, and Hannah looked up sharply.

"I don't know if that's a good idea, Ray."

Rayanne dropped her fork. "Why not?"

"Dogs are dangerous –"

"You can't say that about all dogs, just because you had a bad experience *once*," Ray argued. "And I could volunteer at a reputable shelter, with nice, rabies-free dogs. I won't get attached to anyone, I promise."

Hannah pursed her lips and glanced at Cal. He shrugged and gave her a look that said *your call*.

Hannah glanced from her husband to her daughter.

"If *one dog* steps foot in this house –"

"Paw –"

"Jordie."

"Strictly animal-free house. Got it." Rayanne gave her mom a tight smile. There was a beat as Hannah gave Jordie a look, then she looked at Ray for a long moment.

"All right," she finally relented. "But be careful, Ray, for God's sake. Animals can be unpredictable."

Rayanne didn't have to fight not to roll her eyes. Instead, she grinned, even if the action seemed to take more effort than she remembered.

chapter six

AFTER THOROUGH RESEARCH, and an orientation shift that wasn't as boring as it sounded, Rayanne was set up as a volunteer at a no-kill shelter outside of the city. Brackish countryside and horse farms surrounded the small, brick building; as Rayanne drove down the dirt roads, she always felt a sense of calm. As if in a past life, she'd been a woman who rode horses and smelled like wind.

Outside of the building were enclosed runs for the dogs to play in. Exercising the more docile and trusting rescues was Rayanne's main job, along with cleaning up after them.

For perhaps the first time in years, time passed easily. The open silence of the fields, and the smell of dying leaves and oncoming winter somehow allowed her space to breathe.

Dogs – all mixed breeds, starting with Husky or Shepherd or Lab – would wag their tails and lean into Ray's legs, looking at her with warm brown and hazel eyes. Like they could actually see Rayanne underneath all the bullshit she had made of herself. And they liked her; they thought she was more than enough.

On her fourth shift at the shelter, Rayanne closed the kennel door of an over-excited Malamute, who whined at her sadly.

"I know, baby," Ray whispered to her. "I'll come see you again, before I leave. Okay?"

The dog tilted her head. Rayanne forced herself not to look back too often as she walked out of the large dog ward to wash her hands and "disinfect" before taking out another dog.

When she pushed through the heavy door to the shelter corridor, she came eye-to-eye with Josh Reid. He was just pushing through the cat ward's door, forehead scrunched in a frown, but when he saw Ray his expression smoothed out in surprise.

"Hey," he said. Ray always liked how he said that word: like it was some inside joke or secret only they knew, instead of something everybody said to everyone.

"Hey," she said back, though her voice cracked a little on the word. She swallowed self-consciously, and an awkward silence passed. Josh fidgeted.

"Don't take this the wrong way," he said after a second, "but I sort of had you pegged as an SPCA supporter."

Rayanne smiled at her shoes. "I looked into it, but... Mom was paranoid the dogs there would somehow be scarier. Private school versus public, I guess?"

"Gotta avoid the punks, huh?" Josh asked, totally buying into the stupid analogy. Ray smiled wider.

"Something like that."

Josh smiled, too. Ray pulled at the leash that was still

wrapped around her hands.

"I didn't really expect to see you here, either," she admitted.

"My aunt, with the horses? Her place is up the road. She knows the owners," Josh explained.

"Ah." Ray remembered Josh mentioning his mom's sister a few times. "You had connections."

"Basically." Josh shrugged, like having your Auntie know someone at a dog shelter was actually cool. Which Ray was aware it wasn't, but for once somebody wasn't watching her spaz out about dogs like she was some stupid kid. Josh's hoodie was covered in dog hair, just like hers, and he probably smelled like peroxide and bleach when he got home too.

"Well, seeing as how we're both here," Josh made a frown, like he was actually just thinking this as he said it, "you wanna walk some mutts together?"

Rayanne smiled, and nodded. Josh grinned and gestured to the ward doors.

"Next question: large or small?"

Rayanne didn't even have to think. "Large."

To her absolute delight, Josh beamed. "All right," he said approvingly, holding out a closed fist. Rayanne reached out and bumped hers against it lightly.

She knew to anyone else, maybe other girls, the gesture would have seemed obviously platonic. Like a snub, almost; something guys did with friends. But somehow, it didn't feel that way at all.

Rayanne pushed into the large dog ward after Josh, feeling the sleeves of their hoodies brush and catch against one another.

AS A SHEPHERD-CROSS sprinted ahead toward the trees with an unsuspecting crow in his sights, Rayanne snuck a glance over at Josh. They walked with their hands in their pockets, denying the oncoming winter by lifting their faces to the fading sunlight, too bright for the fading season.

"So how've you been?" Josh asked.

Rayanne fixed her gaze on the dirt grooves in the field, worn by tractor tires.

"Okay. I guess."

Josh's accepting nod seemed like confirmation; only with him, did her stilted half-answers feel like enough, even if just for now.

WHEN HANNAH BROUGHT her cup down forcefully on the dinner table, Rayanne jumped. The passive outburst wasn't directed at her, but Rayanne still felt it vibrate through her bones. She could feel Hannah's anger radiate into the air like waves, but it wasn't anything new. And this, she pondered, could be why she needed the "coping mechanisms" Ms Boyer kept talking about. The words felt clunky to Rayanne. She'd swear backwards and forwards that her life wasn't bad, that she didn't have any traumas that needed coping with. Really, it was the truth.

Rayanne looked at her food: cooked carrots, baked tofu and rice. She separated the carrots into pairs and then pushed the rice into a perfect circle. She wasn't sure if Hannah's and Cal's fighting was a good or a bad thing, she just knew that everyone's parents did. Still, it was hard to feel her heartbeat quicken at her mother's raised voice and think *it's okay, this is normal.*

Rayanne wasn't sure what other parents' fights looked or sounded like. She imagined broken dishes and slamming doors. In her house, Hannah was always the one shouting hysterically, while Cal chose his words like sharpened blades. Their fights meant *noise* – they meant toxic airwaves that cloaked Rayanne like a second skin which she wore around for days.

When she was younger, the fights were always between Hannah and Cal. But as Rayanne grew up, the conflicts were more often than not between Hannah and Amy.

"I'm just saying," Amy reasoned, and Rayanne could actually feel her sister fighting to keep her tone level, "that if Dmitri got away with wearing that hoodie that said *kush nugs* at Thanksgiving, then I shouldn't have to censor myself, either."

Rayanne laid her tofu out in a perfect line. She barely remembered Thanksgiving: sneaking most of her food to her grandma's toy poodle, Cocoa, and still purging in the bathroom.

Rayanne felt her throat close up. She stared at the tofu.

"Amy," Hannah sighed and pinched the bridge of her nose. "You have a button on that purse that says 'have a gay day'. It's offensive."

"It's not offensive!" Amy argued for the tenth time. "It's genuine and surrounded by rainbows. *I'm* gay, so it's okay! We're taking the slurs back."

Hannah looked pointedly at Cal. Cal looked at Amy.

"It confuses people. Not everybody is on your level."

Amy glared at her food and muttered, "Everyone should be on my level."

"Well, they're not," Hannah cut in. "Uncle Trev saw Kyle playing with one of those things and he flipped. I don't want to have to apologize for every button on your purse. So either take them off, or bring a different purse. It's your grandmother's house, not the Pride

Center on campus."

Amy's cheeks flushed with anger. Jordie ducked her head; Carina stiffened. Rayanne watched with wide eyes.

"No." Amy was using her Debate Team voice. Never a good sign. "That's the whole point of *pride*, Mom. I'm proud of who I am."

Amy and Hannah stared each other down. A deadly beat of silence passed, the implications of Amy's words settling around the table.

"I'm proud of you, Amy." Hannah's voice didn't exactly back up this statement. "It's just your buttons…"

Rayanne swallowed hard. She'd eaten four carrots and two spoonfuls of rice, and knew she couldn't stomach more.

"No, which is it?" Amy retorted, "You have a problem with the buttons, or me? You weren't exactly supportive when I brought Kate around."

"Well, you and Kate didn't last long, honey, so I don't see why you mind."

"That's *so* not the point." Amy crossed her arms.

Rayanne's hands slid under the table. She pressed her fingernails into her wrist, hard enough to burn like a tiny flame.

"Amy, you can't talk to your mother like that," Cal warned.

Carina's hand slid over Rayanne's under the table, pulling her hand away. The burning pain against her wrist eased, but the anxiety returned.

"This is unfair and you know it!"

"Take the buttons off. Just for suppers at your grandma's. What's that? One meal every few weeks?"

"One meal where I pretend to be someone else, *again*."

Carina slid her plate a little closer to Rayanne's, her eyes flicking up to her sister's. Rayanne leaned forward, just subtly, while sliding her plate closer to Carina's.

"You don't have to pretend anything." Hannah's voice rose again. "For God's sake, nobody suspects you of being straight."

Amy's mouth dropped open. "What the hell does *that* mean?"

Silence. Hannah's shoulders drooped, regret already showing in her features. Amy stood up from the table abruptly. Her fork dropped to her plate with a sharp clatter as she left the kitchen, and a moment later, the front door slammed.

Cal sighed. Hannah dropped her head into her hands. Jordie looked up at Carina and Rayanne uncertainly, but Rayanne couldn't think of anything reassuring to say.

When she glanced down at her plate, Rayanne saw that her tofu and rice were both gone. A last bite of tofu still lingered on Carina's fork, though for the life of her, Rayanne couldn't remember if her sister even liked tofu.

October 18
> *I think I was born with some kind of factory setting that has me believing it's healthy to assume everything is somehow my fault.*

THE NEXT AFTERNOON, Rayanne hurriedly pulled her books out of her locker. The hallway behind her was already empty. She was five minutes late for her fourth period chemistry class. Instead of spending another lunch hour pretending to eat, she had opted to hang out with Josh and Cameron out by the soccer fields. She could still feel the warmth of the October sun, and hear the music from

Josh's iPod.

When her chemistry textbook sprang free, it sent a small stack of papers floating down onto the floor.

Cursing under her breath, Rayanne knelt down and gathered the paper. A small, rectangular card caught on the soft skin of her palm. She picked it up and turned it to the front, suddenly realizing she had taken it from Ms Boyer without reading it over.

Apparently, Hannah had joined forces with the counsellor to get Rayanne back into the routine of annual doctor's visits. Ms Boyer said she had connections at a clinic downtown.

Rayanne had taken the card with her appointment time, but then stuffed it into her locker and promptly pushed the topic out of her mind.

Now, she stared in cold dread at the neatly printed letters:

Fourth Avenue Women's Clinic
Dr. Biri, M.D.

Then, in smaller print:

Specializing in the treatment of Eating Disorders and disordered eating.

Rayanne blinked, but the words remained the same.

Quickly, she stuffed the card and papers back into her locker and slammed the door. Her footsteps echoed through the empty hall as she walked away.

IT TOOK ONLY TWO WEEKS for Rayanne to log her mandatory hours at Forever Home. She kept going.

The girl who worked evenings was a tough twenty-something brunette named Riley. Rayanne liked her because she wasn't interested in small talk, and like

Rayanne, only seemed to enjoy conversation when it was about the dogs.

Rayanne walked into the shelter on an already dark Wednesday evening, the smell of bleach disinfectant itching her nose. Riley looked up from behind the cramped reception desk.

"Hey dude. I hoped you'd be in today."

"I wrote my name on the schedule." Rayanne headed for the door that led back to the kennels.

"Right. I forgot to look." Riley's eyes were fixed on the desk's ancient computer screen. "I need your help with Echo. She had a rough day."

Rayanne froze. She turned to Riley.

"Rough how?"

"A truck from the city came to empty the dumpster behind the runs." Riley spoke as her fingers flew across the computer's keys. Ray wondered how she could talk and type at the same time. "You know how she is with loud noises. She hasn't moved in hours, and she won't eat."

"Okay," Ray said, pushing through the door. "I'm on it."

Echo was a German shepherd cross, who, as far as Rayanne knew, let exactly two people close enough to touch: Riley, and the shelter owner, Diane. A neglectful and abusive home meant she only tolerated humans, at best.

Rayanne thought Echo was beautiful. But she'd always admired the dog from afar, trying to be respectful of her need for space.

As Rayanne approached a tucked-away, chain-linked run in the large dog ward, she saw Echo curled into a ball at the very back. Her long, brown-then-black coat shimmered as she trembled. Dark dimples above her eyes moved with every twitch of soulful, hazel eyes. Her ears, usually pricked above her head and a little floppy, lay flat.

Her chin was mere inches above the concrete floor; her collection of blankets lay forgotten in the corner. Rayanne had noticed how the dog denied herself simple comforts, and she wondered if this was normal for animals. She couldn't fathom a reason a malnourished, cold dog would prefer concrete over cotton blends – even if they were secondhand. Was the softness too unfamiliar?

Instead of opening the gate, Rayanne knelt in front and clasped her hand in the chain-link. Echo watched her without a sound.

"It's okay, baby," Rayanne crooned. "Did the garbage truck scare you? I know, loud noises are scary."

Echo's tail twitched. Taking this as encouragement, Rayanne stood and slowly entered the dog run.

Once she latched the door behind her, Rayanne didn't move to the back of the run, but just knelt down on the concrete. Echo's water and food dishes were both full, but untouched. Rayanne pushed them to the side.

"Let me tell you a secret," she whispered, settling onto the concrete. "Nobody – absolutely nobody – can make you eat if you don't want to."

Echo rested her chin on the concrete and sighed.

"I dunno. That always comforts me." Rayanne looked at her nails. They had a slightly blue tinge, like dying flames.

For a while, they just sat. Rayanne had no idea what to do with rescue dogs. She just sensed that this was a sort of meet-in-the-middle situation, and that it would take some time, if it worked at all.

Loud noises did this to Echo pretty often. And usually Riley would be the one sitting with the dog until she eventually crawled over and ate food out of Riley's hand – as if after all that trauma, being fed was better than eating alone.

Riley must have been busy, or have run out of patience, to delegate this responsibility to Rayanne. Still, she felt honored.

Rayanne reached over and began to smooth out the blankets, getting Echo hair all over the sleeves of her coat in the process. She didn't care.

"See?" Rayanne patted the blankets. "They're soft. Warm. Good, right?"

Echo lifted her head with interest, but it was more for Ray's voice than the blankets. Ray smiled and rubbed her hand over the fabric.

"Come on, sweetie. Come off the hard floor."

Still shaking, Echo crawled onto the blankets. She didn't lie down, but sort of hovered.

Rayanne sighed. She wondered what it must feel like to be terrified all the time; the dog's muscles must be so stiff, just from shaking.

Rayanne waited. Slowly, Echo let herself settle down onto the blankets. Rayanne smiled and let her head fall back and rest gently on the brick wall. She closed her eyes.

That's when she realized: it was *quiet*. She knew enough about working in a dog shelter to recognize it for the rarity it was. Forever Home had just over sixty rescues, a third of them youngsters; there was almost always someone howling, yapping, whining, or barking somewhere.

Not that night. If Ray had been counting, she would've seen ten minutes pass, then fifteen and then twenty, where nobody made a sound at all. For once, though, she wasn't counting the minutes. She just sat and thought of the other dogs lying in their kennels, enjoying this collective peace.

There was a soft, warm weight against Ray's thigh, as Echo curled into the blankets. She could feel the line of the dog's back pressing gently into the fabric of her jeans. As Echo sighed, the breath pushed against Ray and she sighed, too.

chapter seven

DR. BIRI SETTLED herself on the tiny stool across from Rayanne. "Rochelle told me we had some difficulty with the weigh-in today."

"She did it wrong."

"A person's weigh fluctuates naturally, every day," Dr. Biri explained. "All I need is an approximate number. Is your weight a sensitive topic for you?"

"Not when it's taken correctly."

"Or when it's the right number?" Dr. Biri raised her eyebrows. Rayanne said nothing. "Ray, I'm not here to interrogate you. We're here because your family is concerned about you. I want to help."

Dr. Biri asked Rayanne questions similar to ones she'd been asked by Ms Boyer. Then the usual, too-personal questions that doctors always asked. When she was finished, she stepped out of the exam room and returned with Hannah. Hannah offered her daughter a tight smile.

"Mrs. Timko," Dr. Biri said, "based on what I've learned today, I believe that your daughter fits the criteria for an eating disorder."

Rayanne's gut twisted. Edie gave a vindictive grin but Ray could feel her panic – she was terrified of being stopped, of being ripped away from Rayanne like a tumor, leaving her bloody.

"There are resources available to help her, and your family," Dr. Biri continued. "I'll refer her to a therapist who specializes in young girls with anorexia – she is quite good – but it may take a while to get an appointment. Rayanne will be put on a waiting list."

"What are we supposed to do until then?" Hannah's voice was quiet, almost pleading.

"She can continue seeing her counsellor at school. And I would like to see Ray more often, to check in with her vitals. I just want to be sure her health doesn't nosedive any farther."

Hannah sniffed. Her eyes were watery, but she didn't cry. "And what if it does?"

The delicate lines around Dr. Biri's eyes deepened. "Then we'll have to look at hospitalization."

Cold fear washed over Rayanne's shoulders.

RAYANNE HAD NEVER liked people looking at her. She'd hide behind her classmates at Christmas recitals, would turn beet red at every *Happy Birthday* sung in her honour, and avoided cameras at all costs; she even attempted to skip picture day twice.

Still, as a young girl, there'd always been something special about a *dress*. They were pretty and soft and they meant she was going somewhere exciting. Of course, by the end of the night, five-year-old Rayanne was inevitably tucked away in some corner, trying with all her might to tear her annoying pair of tights off her legs.

As she stood in Jenny's Bridal near the end of October, Rayanne was certain she'd never hated a piece of clothing more in her entire life.

The saleslady, Maureen, had the coldest hands Ray had ever felt, aside from her own. She could feel each brush of the woman's skin against her back as she laced up the bodice of the bridesmaid dress. Rayanne perched studiously, clasping the front of the bodice to her chest with shaky hands.

There was a mirror in front of them. Rayanne stared at her feet.

"See, this is why this bodice is *so* handy," Maureen said. "No alterations. You just *pull* –" she tugged violently at the ribbon. Ray jerked and Edie took a sharp inhale. "Until it fits."

She tied the bow and stepped back. Behind Ray, on the couches, were Tatiana and the rest of her bridesmaids. Ray could feel their eyes like ants across her skin.

"Well come on, give us a twirl!" Maureen demanded, and Ray turned slowly on the spot.

Relief rushed through her when the action was met with appreciative sighs. Tensing, she glanced in the mirror. The bodice was pulled tight around her rib cage, and her collar bones were stark beneath the store's washed-out lighting.

She put up with her mother's insistence to twirl the skirt, and Maureen's tendency to reach out and tug at the fabric. While Tatiana talked things over with her Maid of Honour and mother, frantic about the skirt length, Ray felt beads of sweat begin to develop on her forehead.

90 pounds, Edie reminded her.

I'm five away.

Five pounds? Might as well be fifty. The drop of the fabric shows the fat on your stomach. See? Edie sneered. Rayanne looked in the mirror. She saw.

Jesus, look at you – sweating bullets. You can barely handle a dozen people looking at you, how are you going to handle a whole wedding ceremony?

chapter eight

CARINA DEVOURED MAGAZINES. Her closet had a bookcase full of them and she was the only person Rayanne knew who visited Chapters for the mag stand, not the books. Her favourites were *Kinfolk, Nylon, Vanity Fair* and *Dwell*.

Rayanne couldn't remember what exactly had compelled her to pass the time by reading Carina's latest issue of *Cosmopolitan*. It was one of the trashier magazines, in Ray's opinion, but at least knowing that going into it offered her some sort of justification.

Halfway through, she came to a photograph of a young model at the end of a runway in that typical model pose: one hand on her bony hip, the other held slightly out, as if drawing attention to the fact that her body was actual, technical art. She had straight, long blond hair and blood red lips, round like a cherry. The dress she wore was lace.

Rayanne was about to turn the page when the tiniest imperfection caught her eye. Squinting, and bringing the photo a little closer to her face, Ray could make out dozens of tiny healed cuts on the inside of the model's arm. They were pale and puckered, nearly invisible.

Ray stared, unable to believe what she was seeing. But the photo was just a runway snapshot, not a sleek photoshoot; no Photoshop-trained eyes had been turned on it. A photographer at a fashion show had managed to capture a girl's most glaring vulnerabilities – and nobody had noticed.

Rayanne cut the picture out of the magazine and stuffed it between a couple of paperbacks on her bookshelf.

ON THE FIRST WEDNESDAY of November, Rayanne had been talked into spending lunch hour with Charmayne and Madison. After choking down half of her dad's packed lunch, she'd shut herself away in the school's bathroom and purged as much as she could.

After school, she found herself sitting on the ground against her bed. Her journal was lying just a little ways away, but she couldn't even look at it.

In her hand was a thick permanent marker and she was only half aware of the movements her hand was making. Scrawled across her right leg was the word "UGLY." On her stomach, "FAT". Now, she slowly wrote the word "WEAK" on the inside of her left wrist.

She hummed steadily the tune of Brahms's Lullaby. It calmed her and she feared that if she stopped, she would put down the marker and find something sharper to press against her skin.

Carina came into their room, talking over her shoulder, but when she turned and saw Ray, she froze. The books in her arms dropped to the floor.

Ray opened her mouth to say something, even though she had no idea what could possibly come out. It didn't matter. Carina turned and sprinted up the stairs.

Ray let the marker drop to the ground and buried her face in her hands.

Footsteps, two pairs this time, descended the stairs. Carina appeared with Amy right behind. Ray didn't know whether to be grateful that today was the day she did her laundry at their house. Amy's eyes were steely as she took in the sight of Ray on the floor. She knelt down and grabbed Ray's arm, inspecting the ink. She licked her hand and began rubbing the word furiously, but all it did was blur the edges slightly.

"Why are you writing on yourself?" Amy's voice was surprisingly even. Ray looked down, feeling the blood rise to her cheeks in shame. Amy grabbed the marker, put the cap on, and chucked it across the room.

"...Bad day." Ray pulled her sleeve down to cover her wrist. Amy looked to Carina – for reassurance, maybe – but she just shook her head wordlessly.

They sat on the couch and watched TV, trying to go back to normal. A mindless reality show was enough to distract Rayanne for a while. Cal came home from work, then Hannah; Amy drove back to her place on the East Side.

By nightfall, Rayanne had almost forgotten about the incident. So when she pushed her sleeves up to help with emptying the dishwasher, she ended up exposing her marked arm.

Hannah's eyes landed on the word etched into Rayanne's skin, and Ray knew she was in deep.

In every fight she could ever remember having with her parents, it seemed that Hannah was the one yelling while

Cal was the one standing in the back, solemnly nodding his head.

It didn't happen that way, that night. Hannah held a confrontational stance, her arms crossed and her brow knit together as she stared Ray down, but no words came out of her mouth.

Cal faced away from them, his own arms crossed as he stared out the side door to the sunroom.

They didn't hand out punishments. They didn't say they were disappointed. For the first time, Hannah was silent, chewing on the inside of her cheek.

The minutes stretched on as Rayanne pulled at her sleeves and shivered on one of the kitchen chairs.

"I don't...understand."

Rayanne was shocked when Cal spoke first. Hannah must have been, too, because she jumped slightly and turned to look at him.

His voice was quiet but it wasn't calm. It held a tremor, a suppressed anger that startled Ray because it was so uncommon. He turned to face Ray, and she realized her dad looked older than she remembered. There were lines around his eyes, and flecks of grey in his beard. "I don't understand. Do you not have a good home here?"

Ray felt every pint of blood drop to her feet and tears sprang to her eyes.

Don't you dare cry, Edie threatened. Ray pressed her lips together.

"Your mom and I are good parents. We love you girls a lot. You have a good school." As he talked, Cal's voice became more strained with emotion. "You have good lives. So I don't understand."

He just looked at her. He expected her to answer.

"Understand what?" she croaked.

"What about this is so hard that you need to act this way? Are you trying to punish us?"

Tears streamed down Ray's cheeks and she tried to suck in a breath. It didn't help when she saw that her mom was crying too.

Edie turned away in disgust.

"No." It was the truth.

"I don't understand where we went wrong." Cal looked at Hannah.

A sob broke through Ray's throat. "You didn't -"

"Well something went wrong." Cal's voice was beginning to get louder as he gestured to Ray, to her shrunken body hiding beneath an oversized sweatshirt. "Why else would you do this to yourself?"

She didn't have any answers.

She sat there and willed the tears to stop, detesting that small sign of weakness. Her dad let out a rough breath and left the kitchen, walking down the hall and slamming his bedroom door behind him.

chapter nine

RAYANNE CRAVED SLEEP more than anything, possibly even food. The promise of closing her eyes and being able to rest, for a while to not be her, with that mind and those problems and the body that she only knew how to hate so much, was too good to be true. Which is why she never got it.

The house was quiet, almost peaceful. The clouds had tapered off and a slice of moon lit the world enough to shine through Ray's postage stamp window. Everyone was sleeping, Carina's breathing was shallow and rhythmic across the room, and Jordie's music from upstairs had turned off hours ago. Restless, Ray crept quietly out of bed. She pulled on an extra sweater and a pair of slippers then walked slowly upstairs, avoiding the parts of the floor that she knew creaked.

Dead leaves from the surrounding trees had settled on top of the sunroom, and they cast shadows on the carpeted floor. Moonlight spilled on the glass's dusty surface. Besides an old dirty lawn chair and a few empty clay pots, the room was empty.

Not caring about the dirt, Rayanne collapsed into the lawn chair.

Are you trying to punish us?

Her dad's words rattled around in her brain, as clear as if she were hearing them for the first time. Now, hours after the fact, she had begun to come up with something close to an answer:

It wasn't supposed to be this way. Everything in her life was supposed to be better when she was thinner. She was supposed to be more confident, have more friends, be smarter, more beautiful, more happy. She hadn't meant to hurt anyone.

She didn't know how long she stayed there, watching the eerie shadows of leaves and branches stretch across the glass as the moon moved. She regarded the clay pots in the corner.

Just then, Ray heard the smallest creak coming from the kitchen, but in the night it was so loud she almost jumped out of her skin. She twisted to look through the door, which stood halfway open.

In the faint light she saw Cal shuffling past the kitchen island. She held her breath and quickly leaned out of view of the doorway, but not so much that she couldn't see into the kitchen.

Cal got a glass from the cupboard and filled it with water from the pitcher inside the fridge. Ray noticed he didn't look as if he had just woken up, but as if he too hadn't slept.

He took a few sips of his water, staring at the cupboards in front of him. When he drained his glass, he set it on the counter and twirled it a few times with his fingers.

Then, Cal's shoulders slowly hunched. Leaning forward, he lowered his head and rested his face in his hands.

Rayanne's skin prickled when he stayed that way for many moments. It was such an unusual, vulnerable posture. His shoulders shook slightly, but he didn't make a sound. Then suddenly he straightened up and took a deep breath. He set his glass in the sink, ran a hand over his face once, and turned away. Ray didn't make a noise as he slowly walked back down the hallway to his and Hannah's room.

November 10
I am a waste of space. Maybe that's why my brain is so obsessed with making me take up the least amount of it as possible.

THE NEXT DAY, on the way home from the shelter, Rayanne stopped at Canadian Tire. Their garden section was pitiful beneath the fluorescent lights, November snow melted in puddles on the floor near the bags of soil. Rayanne waded through the post-summer depression anyway, and bought potting soil, plant food, pots, and seeds.

The plants were called *mandevilla*, and they promised white blooms and creeping vines. Ray imagined what they would look like wild and grown, crawling up toward the sunlight like arms.

In the sunroom, Ray busied herself with organizing the pots and measuring out potting soil. She planted six seeds, though she wasn't sure why that number. When she was done, the pots lay in an expectant row beside the sunroom's glass pane, where she left them for the night.

The next morning, before anyone else was up, she found them sitting in morning sunlight. She could almost sense the life stirring beneath the pungent dirt.

Rayanne closed her eyes, breathed in and smiled.

HANNAH SEEMED to have decided that her best weapon in all of this, while Rayanne was on the waiting list, was organization. She added Rayanne's appointments and sessions to the family calendar, scratched in blue bubbly letters beside Jordie's volleyball practices and Carina's year book meetings.

Time slots, handouts and neon post-it reminders acted as her armour. She'd print out articles on "healthy eating" and the food pyramid and stick them to the fridge with magnets.

Every Thursday morning Hannah reminded Ray that she was seeing Ms Boyer that day. Every afternoon she asked how it went. But the truth of it was, apart from appointment times and other inconsequential anecdotes, Hannah avoided her daughter. She knew when Ray's appointments were but was never there to take her to them; that was a job assigned most often to Amy. Sometimes Ray wondered if she just didn't give it that much thought, but then she would get home and find a new stack of printed-out articles and pamphlets on body-image or ED's or depression. And it was all she could do not to imagine her in the empty house, sitting at her laptop all afternoon reading through them, deciding which ones to print out, wondering if they would help. And then she'd put them on the counter in the kitchen, and Ray would say she'd look through them, but they always sat untouched until Cal carted them out to the recycling bin by the back door.

November 25

I have never, ever believed that I actually deserve to ask for what I need. Even when I was a kid. It didn't matter how mundane something was, or how simple, or how necessary. An extra blanket at sleepovers. A pen when I couldn't find mine at school. Extra ketchup at restaurants. And when I did muster up the courage to ask for these things, I was always left with this terrible residual guilt, this feeling that I was a horrible inconvenience to everybody. And I'm not sure why because it's not like anybody has ever made a point of making me feel that way. It just happens.

There are so many things I need right now. I need to sleep. I need someone to hug me and I need everyone to never touch me again. I need to cry on someone's shoulder without having to explain why I'm crying, because right now, I just can't get into it. I need space and I need contact.

I need every single one of these things at once, yet I don't know how to ask or even if any of them are possible. So I don't say a damn thing, holding out hope that finally, someone will just offer them to me.

ON A FRIGID NIGHT late in November, Rayanne woke up from a nightmare where she did nothing but eat her Baba's perogies and make figurines out of clay. When she woke with a start, it was to her hands flying down to her stomach. The swelling bloat had felt so real, but as her empty stomach shook feebly beneath her palms, she realized it was just a dream.

Once upon a time, she would jolt awake moments before hitting a sudden drop or before a ghost swallowed her whole. Now, she woke in a cold sweat that drenched through her pajamas. The sound of her breathing was loud in the silence of the night around her.

As her eyes adjusted to the dark, Rayanne spied Carina sleeping beneath a mountain of covers across the room. It was a habit she'd picked up as a kid – locating her sister always seemed to ward off memories of bad dreams.

The next day, though, the dream stuck to her like a phantom pain. She tried to flush it out with a steamy shower, so hot it turned her pale skin pink and raw. She stared at the perfect, untouched, white skin on her wrists; the soft blue vein lying beneath. Even with the hot water, every part of her felt numb.

That day she ate a low-fat yogurt and two granny smith apples. She couldn't feel the hunger anymore. When she got home from school she couldn't stop running her fingers across her wrists. She dug her nails into them, hard. The pain started as a burn, rising up to the surface, spreading as she scraped her nails down all the way to her elbow. Angry red lines flared up, ruining the perfect white complexion.

Rayanne smiled. Something about the sensation was satisfying. The burning pain was so simple, she knew what was causing it and she knew how to stop it.

Her eyes flitted to the razor sitting on the edge of the bathtub. It had a purple handle.

The magazine clipping she'd saved of the model with scars on her wrist was still tucked away on her bookshelf, worn from where she would unfold it and look at it, just for a while. The caption gave the name of the dress designer, but not the model. Ray didn't know who she was.

She was beautiful.

Rayanne didn't know why she kept the picture. She should probably throw it out.

Way back when this had started, she thought something about wanting to be light as paper. But now she was wondering why she would want to be something so easily folded up and hidden away, worn from the use of people who knew nothing about who she was.

chapter ten

WHEN RAYANNE WAS a little girl, her favourite month was December for the obvious reason: Christmas. Now, she'd lost track of the months completely and which ones she preferred. All she cared about was being warm, which was getting increasingly harder the thinner she grew.

The scariest part was, she wasn't trying anymore. On a Friday morning she stepped on the scale to be rewarded with the number 89, and she felt hollow. Edie had absolutely nothing to say, but hovered constantly, as if the silent treatment was a twisted sort of reward.

Rayanne should have expected this. It's not like Edie was exactly *kind*.

That Friday afternoon, Josh caught up to her walking numbly to her fifth period class. They'd been talking more at school, gravitating toward each other. From across the hall Rayanne would see her friends watching them.

"Are you busy after school?" he asked her, and Ray

looked up at him.

"Not really." Her mind flashed to the journal she longed to get home to.

"Do you wanna hang out? I wanna take you somewhere."

Rayanne's heart didn't skip, but flat out stumbled, as graceless as she always felt. She forced down a swallow and then said, "Yeah. That sounds good."

Sitting through fifth period was difficult after that. But after what felt like ages, she found herself nestled into the passenger seat of Josh's black Civic. It smelled faintly of weed, dogs and body spray, but Ray liked it.

"So where are we going?" Ray asked, once Josh had pulled away from the school and sped off toward the freeway.

"I told you my dad works construction, right?" He looked over at her, green eyes scrunching up a little. Especially in the winter light, his skin was slightly tanned. Ray wondered if this was some form of bizarre sunshine retention, or if he had darker genes somewhere in his blood.

Ray nodded quickly, hoping Josh hadn't caught her staring at him. She fixed her eyes on the passing city outside.

"He's working at this site across the city. It looks pretty dope at night."

Ray frowned, trying to wrap her mind around this. They were going to a construction site?

"Okay." Ray said. "Cool."

It started to snow. Traffic slowed. Through the speakers, Josh played his iPod: low-fi, indie stuff that Ray didn't recognize but she guessed Amy would.

"You know," Ray said, because she was feeling a little strange, "your taste in music always surprised me."

Josh looked at her, amused. "Why?"

Ray lifted a shoulder. "Hockey boys usually listen to, like…rap music." She put on a ridiculous, masculine voice. "Fight music."

Josh laughed. "Do you always think of me as a *hockey boy*?"

Rayanne blushed furiously, but she wasn't as embarrassed as she would have been with someone else.

"I don't know. Labels are weird?"

Josh thought about this. "Yeah. I hear that."

After a while, with the sun mostly down, they reached a building site on the very eastern edge of the city. It was all part of a new development: brand-new schools were to be surrounded by even newer apartments and condos.

These weren't even condos yet, but just the skeletons of them, wooden boards for walls and thick pillars marking off doorways and corners and the trusses of roofs. They were tall, five or six stories high. The sight was deserted now, the workers having gone home for the night, and it was an eerie sight. Snow fell thick past the staring, soon-to-be windows.

There were single light bulbs at the ends of thick orange cords, surrounded by their own tiny cages. Dozens of them hung from the fresh rafters of every floor. They gave off an ethereal glow against the darkening sky.

Immediately, Rayanne understood why Josh would want to bring someone here.

Josh parked the car and they climbed out.

"Come on," Josh said, grabbing her hand. He led her across the street and through an opening in the construction fence, right into one of the buildings.

"Josh, that sign said we're under video surveillance."

"So?" Josh replied easily. "What's the video going to

show, two teenagers walking around? We're not tagging the place."

They walked through the skeleton building, the lights casting long, eerie shadows against the dirt floor. It smelled like sawdust and snow and their breath rose in the air and caught the yellow-gold light. Ray looked straight up and saw the same pattern in the structure repeated, floor after floor, light after light, until her eyes found a patch of the flimsy tarp that served as a roof. Sporadic snowflakes still drifted down past the wood.

"Ray?" Josh's voice seemed suddenly loud in the quiet air. She turned to look at him, wrapping one arm around a wooden pillar.

"Hm?"

"You're going to university after we graduate. Right?"

Ray frowned, thinking this was a very random question. Josh was staring up through the wood beams.

"That's the plan. I don't know what I'm going to study, though. Why?"

He shrugged, looking at her. "I just have this weird feeling like you're leaving. Like I'm going to have to say goodbye, or something."

Rayanne shivered, but she blamed it on the cold. "I'm not leaving. At least, not that I know of." She walked a little ways down the building, stepping up onto the frame of what would be a door in the future. She wrapped her arms around either side of the frame.

"Okay. Good."

She frowned, confused by Josh's serious voice. "What's going on, Josh?"

"I've just been thinking a lot," he said, quietly, "About how I kind of just left you. I feel really shitty about that."

Ray looked down, her chest tightening as she struggled

59

to keep control. "It's okay."

"No it's not," Josh said simply. "I really liked you – I still like you – but then. I dunno, I guess I just didn't know how to handle it."

Rayanne nodded. She tried not to say *it's okay* again. "I like you, too."

The words were so simple, and kind of childish, but right then they were perfect.

Josh walked toward Ray until there were inches between them. She stood frozen, her arms on either side of the doorframe.

Rayanne suddenly got the strangest sensation that she was a figure inside a snow globe – frail and perfect, frozen in time, surrounded by stars and golden light and the snow settling on their shoulders. She didn't want this moment to break.

Josh asked, "Do you remember when we first hung out, and you were chilling with Tucker?"

Ray thought. "Yeah. We were at the rink, right? He kept me warm. I loved that dog."

"I remember the way you were looking at him. Like you trusted him, right away. And I just got this feeling... I wanted you to look at me like that."

Love and want rushed up in Ray at the same time, and Josh took that last step, closing the distance between them. She could feel her pulse quicken when he leaned in, and he hesitated for a single beautiful moment, his soft lips brushing against hers, before he actually kissed her.

Warmth tingled everywhere. Josh brought his hand up to her face, entwining his fingers gently in her hair. Warmth exploded into heat, and Ray understood then how a person could melt.

She didn't know how long it took for them to break

apart, but when they finally did, it still felt like too soon. Ray's breathing had quickened and the maddest hope filled her heart, her veins, her very limbs. But that couldn't stop the alarmed voice from whispering repeatedly in her head, *What have you done?*

THAT NIGHT, RAYANNE lay awake brushing her fingers against her lips.

Was she Josh's girlfriend now? Did he want that?

Tatiana's wedding loomed. In just over twelve hours she would be walking down the aisle of a cathedral painted with angels. The pews would be creaking under the weight of not only her entire family, but somebody else's, too. And for fifteen horrible seconds, all their eyes would be on *her*, instead of on the bride or the groom or anybody who deserved the attention.

It suddenly hit her that Tatiana was getting married; that someone only a few years her senior had found a person who was willing to stick around forever.

Rayanne had never entertained Princess-esque fantasies about herself and love before. It never interested her or even felt *right*. Now she was suspecting why. While others were natural-born parents or partners, it was possible Rayanne had been born to be alone.

She couldn't do any girlfriend-type activities. She wouldn't go to the movie theatres or have dinner out at a restaurant; wouldn't go out to the beaches in the summer in a bathing suit. Rayanne couldn't be the girlfriend who would share a milkshake with her boyfriend during lunch break on the hot days before summer break.

Who would want to say that their girlfriend sees a therapist? That she has a chart up on her fridge telling her what she must eat for every meal of every day, like a child?

There would be too many lies. Everything she said was a substitution for the truth: reasons to get out of eating, cover-ups for missed sessions and appointments, excuses for being the way she was. And she couldn't stop any of it. *I can't, I can't, I can't.*

Nothing about Ray was functional girlfriend material. She stared at herself in her bathroom mirror until her reflection drooped like a fun house mirror. Nothing was desirable – she was too bony to represent a girl and then too fat to represent a person at all. She was not lovable.

One of the last places Rayanne wanted to be was at a wedding, where this gold standard of *lovable* and *wanted* would be impossible to ignore.

In her bathroom, Rayanne locked the door and turned the shower water on, though she didn't step beneath the stream. Her hands shook only slightly when she brought the razor down, gently, on the skin of her thighs. She was dying to open the skin on her wrists, but the strapless nature of Tatiana's dress meant that she had to wait.

The handle had dried shaving cream on it. It smelled like flowers or maybe some kind of fruit. The blood appeared in tiny bubbles that popped out of her skin. They were almost beautiful: dark paint on a previously perfect canvas.

Something seemed to be shaken loose from Rayanne then. As she stared down at the red on her thighs, she hoped maybe she had been able to free the monster from inside herself at last.

She found her way back to her and Carina's room and dug out her journal. Legs throbbing beneath Band-Aids, she opened to the next blank page and began to write.

I am the bones pressing against my skin. You look at me as if I'm a contagious disease, but you can't stop looking because it's horribly beautiful, in a way. How frail. How delicate.

I am not contagious; this is not something you can catch by touching me. This is all mine. I earned this frailty; I crave it, I feed off it.

I do not want to be like you. You are not like me; you are not strong enough to be thin, you are not smart enough to reach numbers, track numbers, lose numbers. And that makes me happy.

Today I will count. Today I will starve. I will turn into myself like an imploding star. Just like yesterday. I'll stumble through my life because it's the only thing I know. If I don't count and starve and measure and critique, how will I know when I am good enough? How will I know what

Or who

I am?

chapter eleven

THE NEXT MORNING, Rayanne's only plan was to stay in bed indefinitely. It seemed to be, inexplicably, the best laid plan she'd ever had.

Staying there, however, wasn't as easy. By late-morning her cousins showed up with their arms full of bridesmaid dresses, and she knew she was only starting what would probably be one of the longest days of her life.

Ray shivered, but waited patiently as Carina laced up the back of the wine-red bridesmaid dress.

The ribbon kept slipping tighter.

Carina swallowed.

"Were those cuts on your thighs?" she whispered to Ray.

Ray glanced back at her, then around at their cousins. They were all distracted, arguing over music selection and fussing with each others' hair.

"What cuts?"

"On your thighs – I saw when they were messing around with your skirt. What are they from?"

Rayanne's heart was fast as a rabbit's. She thought quickly. "From the pound. I was playing with a rescue cat, and he scratched me."

"Through your pants?" They were still whispering.

Ray lifted one shoulder in a shrug. "They were shitty leggings. They weren't that thick." Carina didn't answer, and Ray had no idea whether she believed her or not; she couldn't see her sister's face.

Tatiana's frantic maid of honour interrupted the group then, and Carina was forced to drop it.

The thing about being in a big family is that Rayanne went to a lot of weddings. Which had its pros and cons, but one of the pros was that she knew exactly what would happen, and what was expected of her.

So she smiled dutifully when she followed slowly, two paces, behind Carina. She stood where the tape was marked in an "x" on the cathedral's floor. She pretended her arms weren't aching from holding that bouquet of flowers.

The groom's side had predominantly pale hair and tall, fit bodies. Rayanne picked out a woman in her sixties whose arm muscles were still toned and visible in her sleeveless dress. Did she do yoga? Pilates?

Rayanne hadn't done yoga in months. She squeezed her stomach muscles tighter, stood up straighter, and compulsively repeated her mantra *think skinny, be skinny*.

When Tatiana turned down the aisle, every head in the crowd turned, and Rayanne allowed herself the tiniest breath of relief.

Afterward – even though snow was falling thickly–everybody wrapped up in their thick coats and boots, and they all walked outside around the church three times (a Ukrainian tradition).

Rayanne was grateful when Carina linked her arm through hers and pulled her close for warmth.

Through the snow, Ray watched the people walking ahead. There were toddlers trampling through snow banks, and little girls lying down to make snow angels no matter what their mothers said.

Ray picked out the couples in the crowd – she recognized distant cousins who had somehow grown older and had people attached to their arms.

But it was strange because while this was her family – while she should belong here – it was as if none of it was actually happening to her. She could describe the patterns of the detailed embroidery on the tablecloths, and the rosy cheeks on wood-carved birds that sat atop the wedding cake. She knew they were real. But she couldn't feel them there.

Sometimes, she doubted whether any of this was real at all. Maybe this was a prolonged hallucination, and she would wake up as a different person with a different life and no recollection of this whatsoever.

Still, as Ray watched the reception proceedings, her eyes wandered to those couples; to the pictures of the newly married couple plastered all around. One of her cousins – what's-her-face-who-dances – was three years younger than Ray, yet she had a pretty good-looking kid sitting with his arm around her.

Their outfits were matching.

"Ridiculous, right?" Carina lifted an eyebrow at Ray.

Ray was attending her cousin's wedding with her non-identical, technically-older twin sister as her technical date, and what's-her-face-who-dances was the ridiculous one.

"Yeah, kinda," Ray agreed, just to say something. Suddenly, all she could think about were Josh's hoodies. How they were faded like he'd had them for years, and he always pulled them overtop of t-shirts that looked newer and clean. Those hoodies smelled a little like smoke but mostly like fabric softener, and they were so *soft...*

You don't need a boyfriend, Edie whispered. *You have me.*

Ray shivered. The only reply she could come up with was *you hurt*.

Edie smiled. *You wanted this.*

And Rayanne didn't say anything. Because she swore she did.

The reception was loud. The thick snow outside turned to a full-on blizzard and everyone started giving mass updates about the storm via their phones.

Rayanne danced when her sisters made her, but mostly took to wandering around the reception hall, admiring the traditional decorations.

"Rayanne Timko." Hannah's stern voice cut through the cacophony of noise. She had sidled up to Rayanne on her way to the bathroom. "I want to see you helping yourself to dinner in the next half hour."

Dread washed over her, but Rayanne pretended to look resigned.

"I will," she lied. Really, she should be grateful. She knew the half-hour time slot was Hannah's compromise, when really her mother probably wanted to pile a plate with cabbage rolls and sausage and watch Rayanne devour the entire thing.

Rayanne went to the bathroom and then danced the polka with Jordie. She could feel her mother's eyes on her as she ricocheted around the reception hall.

Somehow, sometime between the Father-Bride dance and the Best Man's toast, Rayanne found herself at a table filled with nothing but bread. Most loaves were fashioned into braids. Lush, white-then-brown dough weaved in and around itself. Some loaves were glazed with egg white and reflected the reception's low light; others were peppered with rock salt or poppy seeds.

It was beside these platters of bread that Ray found a *matryoshka* – a nesting doll.

She reached out and picked it up, turned it slowly in her hands.

Rayanne slowly opened each nesting doll, finding a smaller one inside. They stopped after six, and after that she found nothing – it just ended with the smallest nesting doll, sanded clean in half and grooved to fit back together.

Frowning, she glanced around at the discarded halves of nesting dolls. She didn't understand the purpose of it; what good they were besides fancy decoration, if they did nothing but produce smaller and always empty versions of themselves.

Carina appeared at her side, out of breath after dancing with Amy. Now, what's-her-face-who-dances was a part of an entire troop of Ukrainian dancers who were positioning themselves out on the dance floor.

"Mom says you're supposed to grab a plate of food and go back to the table."

"I have ten minutes left."

"Don't start a thing, Ray."

"It's not a thing-" Ray started, but Carina cut her off.

"Look, I know those scratches weren't from a cat – you never choose cats over dogs."

Get on the defensive, Edie advised.

"I don't know what you want me to say."

"Just – be good for tonight, okay? But after this, we all need to sit down and have a talk. Soon. I can't keep covering for you, Ray."

With that, Carina turned and walked away, pulling her phone out of her bra strap as she went.

Two seconds later, Hannah arrived and actually escorted Rayanne through the buffet line. She watched in horror as her mom assembled for her a modest helping of perogies, bread, and a salad comprised mostly of cabbage. Then she was made to sit down at the table between Hannah and Cal.

This is tricky. Edie's dark eyes flicked back and forth between Ray's parents. *Eat slowly, and the smallest bites. Throw the plate away at the first opportunity. Then go to the bathroom and throw it all up –*

Here? The reception hall was packed with people, and the public bathrooms didn't exactly offer up much privacy. Rayanne knew for a fact the women's bathroom was constantly filled with women primping themselves in front of the mirror.

There's a smaller bathroom near the fire exit. I don't think anyone knows about it.

Ray's jaw flexed as she looked in the direction of the fire exit. The bathroom was tucked away in a corridor, near the back doors where people would occasionally step out to have a cigarette.

And she knew it was her best option.

Carefully, she dragged the biggest pieces of cabbage away from the salad and scraped the dressing off with her fork. Then, she gave a single shuddering breath against her raging anxiety and put the greens in her mouth.

Her taste buds immediately jumped – *food* – but this only made the anxiety spike further. And the anxiety made

Ray eat faster, because the quicker this was over, the better. But before she knew it, half of the cabbage salad and a whole perogie had disappeared off her plate.

Luckily, it was right around then that Hannah and Cal decided to go have a dance. Ray wasted no time in dumping her plate in the nearest garbage bin and retreating to the lesser-known bathroom.

Inside, one stall didn't have a door, and the counter was flooded with soapy water. Ray made it to the farthest stall and slammed the door.

Her pitiful stomach felt swollen and cramped. She wanted that food out of her so bad, she could've cried.

Luckily, her hair was already braided, pinned up and fixed with hairspray. So all she had to do was bend over the toilet, press her longest fingers to the back of her throat and wait for it all to be over.

But...

Would it? Be over?

What kind of question is that? What's taking you so long? The more the food sits, the more calories are absorbed...

Ray knelt in front of the toilet. Squeezing her eyes shut, she plunged her fingers down her throat. When her gag reflex protested, she just pressed harder.

Lumps of just-chewed food fell into the toilet. Ray gagged and coughed, ignoring the burning pain in her throat and the tears streaming from her eyes.

Almost over, we're almost there, you're doing so well...

Nearly all of the food Ray ate was in the toilet. But there was still more, she knew it, so she pushed her fingers deeper.

Her nails caught on her throat.

Muscles spasmed and Ray's body rocked; she gagged

violently, tears were pulled from her eyes, and she threw up more...

"Ray?" Jordie's voice echoed around the bathroom.

Rayanne stared, shocked, at the blood sitting in the toilet bowl. She wiped her mouth with the back of her hand. It came away streaked with red.

High-heels clicked toward the last stall.

"I'm fine," Rayanne said. Her voice came out thick and scratched. "Just give me a sec."

Rayanne turned, and saw that in her distress, she hadn't locked the stall door. She reached for it but then it banged open.

Jordie's face was white, and her eyes widened when she saw Ray, huddled on the floor by the toilet.

Her hand was still covered in sick and blood.

"Oh God," Jordie whispered.

At first, Ray's eyes had just watered from the gagging. But now the tears wouldn't stop.

"I think something's wrong," she said, thinking the words sounded stupid but she didn't know what else to say.

Ray expected Jordie to run for someone, but instead she crouched down beside her and took her face in her hands.

"Where's the blood from?" she asked urgently. Ray's stomach turned.

"I don't know. I think I scratched my throat."

The clicking of more high heels reverberated around the bathroom, and Ray tried to scramble to her feet. Jordie helped.

"Did you find –" Carina's voice started, but then she stopped when she saw Ray. "Is that blood?"

"We think so," Jordie replied quietly.

"Oh, Ray." Carina's brow wrinkled in pain. "Your dress."

Rayanne looked down.

The bodice of Tatiana's bridesmaid dress was spattered with vomit, spit and blood. Spots flecked her vision. "I think I need to sit."

Her knees were shaking. Jordie and Carina helped her to a bench just outside the bathroom door and Rayanne gratefully sat down. They found a coat nearby and draped it around her shoulders.

She was so tired.

"Stay here," Carina ordered. "I'm going to go find Mom and Dad."

Edie was irate, but she didn't say anything. She just glared at Ray. This was her fault.

But, Ray thought, at least she got everything up before they found her.

Jordie sat beside her, crying quietly, and Rayanne couldn't even look at her.

"I think," Jordie tried quietly, but her voice broke. She swallowed and tried again. "I think there's some wash-cloths in the kitchen. Will you be okay if I go get one?"

Ray's chin jerked in a nod, because really, she just wanted Jordie far away – where she couldn't hurt her.

Jordie stood up soundlessly and left.

The doors to outside were propped open to allow air-flow and Rayanne watched the snowstorm rage. It was a study in the contrast of black and white – snowflakes swirled before a black-hole canvas. Rayanne knew, across the cathedral's street, there was a row of residential houses, but she couldn't make out so much as a streetlight.

A figure appeared and she blinked.

Edie stood out there, the blizzard wind whipping at her hair.

Come outside.

Rayanne blinked.

What? You're crazy.

You saw the way Jordie looked at you. And Carrie. You terrify them, you disgust them. Do you want your parents to see you like this?

Rayanne looked out in the direction of the reception hall. She could hear the upbeat tempo of a traditional Ukrainian wedding song, could see the dancers out on the floor.

You're killing them.

Rayanne looked back at Edie.

If you go away, you can't hurt anyone anymore. You won't hurt anymore.

She blinked. And once again, Edie made it sound so easy. So Rayanne shakily stood up and walked to the doorway.

It was like the cold wasn't even surprising anymore.

Shivering, fighting off dizziness, she regarded the storm and decided if anything, at least freezing was simple.

Rayanne left the lights and music behind and stepped out into the storm. The wind was thunderous and tugged at the coat still wrapped around her, so she pulled it closer.

See? Rayanne could hear Edie, underneath the wind. She turned but saw blackness and white swirling snow. She turned again and watched the black sky be swallowed up by a drift of frosty snow, tossed in the wind. Edie was nowhere in sight.

And she had always thought that once she reached a certain number, Edie would pat her on the back and say, *we did it, we're here, you can stop and rest now.*

Rayanne turned back in the direction of the reception hall, but the rectangle of warm light was gone. She walked in the direction of the hall, hoping to see it return. It didn't.

Her knees gave out and she slumped into the snow on the ground.

The world seemed to white itself out, until the only thing that existed was the cold. Her mind flooded with memories of it: cold bathroom tile, chilled steel scale, the cold desks beneath her hands as she shivered in class, cold blankets heaped above her with each waking morning, the cold razor against her skin, Dr. Biri's cold hands, her own blue fingernails, blue veins, blue lips, black eyes, black, blue, white, cold cold cold.

Rayanne realized that she was in the final stages of a grand Disappearing Act. It was what this had been from the very beginning. She had lost so much more than weight. With each pound that slipped away, a tiny part of her life had decayed into the ground.

To be truly gone Rayanne had to leave no traces of herself behind. And so with each pound that left a part of her did too. She lost track of the things she liked or didn't like, of what she was good at and what she found difficult.

She forgot memories that were a part of her heart.

She lost the will to make new ones.

Activities and people and places she used to love or find pleasure in dwindled away into mere sets and props in the act of this disappearing.

How clean and tidy it was. She left no loose ends behind – thanks to Edie, Rayanne was successful in destroying nearly every last relationship that bound her to this earth.

And now this was the final act, she must let go and be swallowed by this endless and inevitable white cold, cold, cold.

Maybe it proved how silly and naïve she had been all along, that she found herself terrified now because she had to complete the thing that she and Edie had set out to do from the very beginning. She had to disappear. What else had she expected to happen?

Something. A small voice whispered it with the wind. Something was supposed to happen.

For the first time, as the wind blocked all noise and Ray became so cold that she didn't feel anything at all, she realized she had been waiting.

This was not a waiting for a certain number or for the right professional to call back. She hadn't been waiting for the right person to say the right thing that might, at long last, break through her walls and help her see reason.

So what was she waiting for?

Her eyelashes were frozen closed, and there were many parts of her body that she could no longer feel, such as her toes and ears and fingers. She felt disembodied, both buried in the winter storm and apart from it, within the cold ground and above it. And suddenly she was terrified – right down to her bones, so much so that she would shake if it were only possible – that she had already died.

It was then that she knew: she had been waiting for Rayanne.

So where was she?

Rayanne clung onto this question with everything she had, desperate for an answer. *Where am I?*

Where am I?

She repeated it over and over again. And somewhere through all of the numb non-feelings of the storm she sensed a warmth across her skin.

I'm right here.

And maybe her mouth formed a smile, or at least tried to, and she knew that she had to sleep for a while because her body couldn't stand consciousness for another second, and after everything Ray had put it through, she knew she owed it this last dying wish.

So she willed herself to let go, the reluctant star performer in this disappearing act. The last thing in her memory was a roaring that she assumed was the sound of her heart stopping and her soul blowing away in the snow.

chapter twelve

HER FINGERS WERE THE FIRST THINGS she felt when she woke up. And they hurt so much that Ray wished she could go back to not feeling them at all.

Why was this happening? Why was there still pain, when she was supposed to be dead?

She groaned without meaning to. The pain was growing. It was unbearable: a sharp hot-burning that throbbed with each pump of blood through her veins. The flames licked every one of her fingers, and a few of her toes.

"Ray? Rayanne?" a familiar voice echoed.

Rayanne opened her eyes and saw nothing but blurry-white.

Snow? Snapshot memories of the storm crashed through her mind; shadows and shapes slid in and out of focus. She opened her mouth to say something but she had trouble finding her voice.

Suddenly, Cal's face appeared above her. It was red and

swollen. His mouth formed Ray's name but this time his voice was too far away for her to hear.

"Dad?" she rasped out, and her hearing snapped back.

"Ray." Cal's voice was relieved.

Other noises found Ray: distant voices, a methodical beeping, and wheels coasting on linoleum. A clean, antibiotic smell filled her nostrils.

It clicked then, she was in the hospital.

"Where's Carrie? Jor –" she started.

"They're here. They're just grabbing some coffee."

Ray swallowed, nodded shakily and tried to push herself up into a straighter position.

That's when she looked down and saw her hands wrapped in thick gauze.

"It's okay." Cal brushed the hair back off Ray's forehead, "They got pretty frostbitten, but they're coming back."

Ray nodded. She'd heard of people getting things amputated from frostbite: fingers, ears, feet...

Ray knew she was lucky.

She inspected her hands. Besides being heavily bandaged, wads of cotton separated her swollen fingers. The skin, where she could see it, was an alarming bright red and there was blistering in places. Her feet were only a little better.

"How are you feeling?"

"Cold." Rayanne tried not to sniffle.

"That's normal, don't worry," her dad reassured her.

Rayanne looked around at her hospital room. There were three beds in it besides hers, only one other occupied, by a snoring man with white hair.

She looked at Cal. "What...uh, how long have I been...down?"

Cal looked at his watch. "Nineteen hours? It's Sunday afternoon."

Rayanne nodded and looked down at her hands.

"I don't think I remember who, uh..." she tried, but her voice quickly failed. She cleared her throat, but it was hard to swallow around the lump there. And that's when Cal dropped his face into his hands and quietly started crying.

To Rayanne's complete and utter surprise, she immediately reached out to him, despite the protesting pain in her fingers.

"Don't – Dad please, don't cry. It's okay; I'm okay," Ray pleaded, and Cal lifted his head and reached for Rayanne's hand, gingerly.

"I'm sorry, I just freaked out." Rayanne's voice sounded thick and garbled. "I didn't know what to do so I freaked out. I didn't mean to. Not just last night, but any of it. I didn't mean to be this way, it wasn't supposed to be like this, I'm sorry I really didn't mean to, I didn't mean to..."

Rayanne hadn't actually cried in what felt like years, but she started bawling then. Cal stood up and wrapped his arms around her.

"I know," he said, stroking her hair. "It's not your fault, Ray. I know."

A few calm, melancholy moments passed as they held one another. Then the relative peace was shattered when Hannah barged into the room.

"This is ridiculous," she said as way of greeting, holding her cell phone in one hand and a coffee in the other. "It's almost noon."

"It's a Sunday –" Cal tried to counter. Rayanne's eyes bounced between them.

"This is her job!" Hannah snapped back. "Is it so unreasonable that I expect to talk to a doctor when my daughter is in the hospital?"

Ray just stared at her, her mouth hanging open in frustration. Maybe Hannah thought her anger was bolstering, but really, it was just stressful. Rayanne wasn't sure why, just that Hannah seemed to be angry for all the wrong reasons.

"I think we should get her a different doctor," Hannah declared.

"No. I like Dr. Biri." Only when she said it did Ray realize it was true.

"It's not her job to make you like her."

"Hannah –" Cal tried to cut in.

"I know, but-"

"I just want to know you're getting the best care – is that so much to ask?"

"No, but Mom –"

"It's been at least an hour since I've even seen a nurse."

"Mom, would you just LISTEN TO ME?"

Ray's voice jumped from her throat, and Hannah stopped short. The silence echoed. She blinked at her daughter, completely taken off guard, and Rayanne asked the question she had not realized was on her mind.

"Why won't you listen to me?" Rayanne's voice was less certain than she would have liked.

"Because I don't understand you." Hannah's voice was just as small. "And that scares me."

"I scare me. But," Rayanne tried to get the words out without crying, "I can't do this if nobody will talk to me. Because nobody's talking, Mom, and it's driving me crazy – I feel like I'm crazy."

Rayanne was crying again, and Hannah rushed over

and gathered her up into a hug.

"You're not crazy," Hannah hushed her.

Rayanne's body felt small and frail crushed against her mom's.

FOR THE NEXT FEW HOURS, Ray sat and talked with her family. They told her about the blizzard. The roof of the old curling rink in Montgomery had collapsed under the snow and a tree had broken on Spadina Crescent, crushing the trunk of an idling car. The North End was still without power, the bridges only just passable.

Throughout these stories, Rayanne watched their faces gratefully. Everyone looked tired, and Jordie's face was as tear-streaked as Cal's.

Carina sat beside her on the bed and she grabbed Ray's hand. She didn't let go for the better part of an hour, even though it hurt her fingers.

Nobody talked about how long Rayanne was staying in the hospital. Nobody talked about how she had ended up there, either. Nurses came and went. They checked the bandages around Ray's fingers and wrote things on the chart by her bed.

They'd also, of course, found the cuts on her legs. Rayanne knew better than to try and lie again.

One of the nurses told her that Dr. Biri would be there in a short while. Rayanne could feel Hannah watching her as she nodded assent.

A little later, Hannah and the girls went home to get some rest, but Cal remained in the chair beside her bed.

At around five a nurse came in with supper: a solitary package of saltine crackers and a bowl of depressing soup. The broth was an acidic yellow, and bits of green herbs floated in it. Rayanne wrinkled her nose at the smell. Twirling it around with the plastic spoon, she spotted bits of chicken floating around with a few slimy noodles.

She dropped the spoon in disgust.

"I'm not eating this."

The white-haired man in the other bed looked over at her, eyebrows raised.

Cal looked up from his magazine.

"Rayanne," he began warily, "I thought we'd discussed –"

"It's chicken noodle. I'm a vegetarian."

Cal set the magazine down, sighing. "I don't think you can afford to be picky, Ray. This is a hospital. And you need food. You don't have the luxury of morals right now – not with the stunt you pulled."

Ray was indignant. "Stunt? Luxury? Dad, look at me. I'm in a hospital, I have no idea when I'll get to go home, my fingers are frostbitten to bloody hell...my morals are all I have left."

Out of the corner of Ray's eye, she saw the old man nodding encouragement.

Cal pursed his lips but didn't say anything.

Ray gestured toward the soup. "You bring me anything without an animal in it – and I'll eat it, I swear I will."

She met her dad's gaze levelly.

After a moment he sighed, held up a finger, and disappeared down the hall. Within five minutes a nurse appeared and took away the Death Noodle Soup, and replaced it with a mushroom barley soup that smelled like angels.

Nope. Absolutely not. Edie crossed her arms stubbornly.

Rayanne brought a spoonful to her lips. The first sensation she felt was *warmth* – it sat heavy on her tongue and then sank down her throat, pooling in her stomach. The savory taste of mushroom exploded on her tongue; the smell of pepper and cream filled her nose. After she swallowed a few spoonfuls, Rayanne closed her eyes and gave a deliberate breath.

Minutes passed slowly in that hospital room. There was a TV, which the white-haired man had turned on, muted the volume, and then promptly fallen asleep in front of. Rayanne passed the time trying to teach herself how to read lips, with absolutely no success.

Throughout all this, she had constant chills. If she sat still long enough, her body would sometimes relax enough to be calm. But as soon as she moved, whether it was to play with the bandages around her hands or to reach for a magazine by her bed, she would stiffen with uncontrollable shaking.

Cal started to fall asleep in his chair, his chin slowly dropping to his chest as snores rose in the back of his throat. Ray woke him up and convinced him to go home and rest.

A little while after he left, Dr. Biri appeared in the doorway. She smiled at Ray before walking past to close a curtain around her bed.

"Hello, Rayanne."

Ray sat up straighter, smoothing the wrinkles out of her sheets. She cleared her throat before replying,

"Hi."

Dr. Biri pulled the armchair a little closer to Ray's bed and sat down.

While Cal had sunk into the chair, Dr. Biri sat perched on the end, Ray's file balancing on her knees. She didn't reach for it.

"So," she said, "I heard you had a rough night."

Ray sort of scoffed but then tried to cover it with a cough. "I guess so."

Dr. Biri took a deep breath. "As you're aware, you've sustained some injuries. You have frostbite on your fingers and toes, but it's mostly superficial. And you were hypothermic when you were brought in, though you're stabilized now. Your temperature is nearly back to normal. That's great. Under normal circumstances you would be going home tonight."

"Normal circumstances," Rayanne mumbled under her breath as she fiddled nervously with her bed sheets.

"Rayanne," Dr. Biri's voice lowered, "when you walked out into the storm last night, were you hoping to die out there?"

Tears welled in her eyes. And once again, she wasn't sure why she was crying, because she was certain she wasn't sad. She answered Dr. Biri with the only truth she knew.

"I don't know if I wanted to die. I just knew I wanted it to stop."

Dr. Biri's forehead creased in sympathy. "That's a very intense feeling to have. But still – recognizing that things need to change, that you can't continue this way, is a huge step."

There was silence. Dr. Biri looked expectant, waiting for Rayanne to accept the bait of a silver lining. Finally, Rayanne gave a solitary nod. Dr. Biri continued.

"I think we can both agree that, at this point, inpatient is the best possible option for you."

"Yeah," Ray agreed, but only because she knew she didn't have a choice. Given the choice, she would sprint down the hall and out the hospital's front doors that second. "How long?"

"Just until your physical health is stable. In your case, I'd say about a week. But the outpatient program is on-going, and can continue for as long as you need it."

Rayanne remained quiet, staring at the points her knobbly knees made in the hospital sheets. Out of the corner of her eye she saw Dr. Biri tilt her head sympathetically.

"I'll come and see you again in the morning," she continued. "And we'll discuss the details with your parents. If my connection comes through, you'll be admitted tomorrow night; Tuesday morning at the latest. Is that alright?"

Ray nodded again, and Dr. Biri reached over and gently placed a hand on her ankle, squeezing slightly.

"I'm proud of you, Rayanne," she said, before rising and leaving the room.

Rayanne was left to stare at the wall opposite. Confusion addled her brain. Because she felt so ashamed and defeated – between treating her family like shit and almost killing herself, she didn't feel like she had done anything even remotely worthy of pride.

ONCE SHE'D GOTTEN some rest, Carina came back and spent the rest of the evening in Rayanne's hospital bed. She brought her books and a stuffed dog toy from the hospital gift shop. They found the TV's remote and watched *Golden Girls*.

"You look better," Carina commented, when Rayanne laughed out loud at a one-liner from Blanche. Carina pressed against Ray's side. "How are you feeling?"

Rayanne tried to put a positive spin on it. "Better, I guess. I'm still cold, but I'm always cold. My hands aren't bothering me as much."

This was true – the pain had been lessening all afternoon,

and a nurse had told Rayanne that she could remove the bandages later that night. She stretched her hands out and wiggled her fingers.

"When are you coming home?" Carina asked quietly and Rayanne froze.

"Not yet," Ray answered, because it was the most honest thing she could think of to say.

There was a beat of silence.

"I think I'm sick," Rayanne said. "At least, they tell me I am. I don't think I am. No, that's not right – sometimes I do feel sick. Or like I'm not right, somehow. And sometimes I feel perfectly fine. I don't know. It's really confusing. But I'm not allowed to leave because they say I'm not healthy enough."

Rayanne let out a frustrated breath.

"But the thing is – I like feeling hungry. I really do. It's an adrenaline rush and it's addicting. And the thing is I know that this isn't healthy – like, if someone else did it, like Jordie or you – I would totally freak out. But I can't see myself that way. When I'm doing it, it doesn't feel unhealthy to me. It feels necessary."

It was the most Rayanne had said to anyone about her disorder, yet it was only the tip of the iceberg; a peek through the keyhole of a giant, padlocked door.

But Rayanne had run out of steam. She fidgeted with the bandages on her hands, and Carina was quiet for a while. Rayanne prayed for her to say something.

"Have you ever done that thing, where whenever you start to get the flu or something, you Google your symptoms?" Carina asked. "Like, you know you're just getting the flu, but you type in that you have a headache and after reading through a ton of articles and blog posts, you're suddenly convinced that you have a cancerous tumor or something."

Carina gave a half-smile, and then kept going.

"Well, that's kind of what I did – when you started looking different. I mean, not just how you looked. The way you acted, too. You weren't as happy or excited about things. You always seemed so tired, and then you started getting thinner. So I Googled it. And I thought it would be like when you Google flu symptoms. Like at first you'd be paranoid that it's this horrible thing, but then time would pass and it would go away and you'd laugh at how you overreacted.

"It wasn't like that, though. Time went by and you didn't get better. Still, all this time I've been in denial, telling myself it's not that bad." She looked up then, around at the walls of the hospital, before resting her gaze on Rayanne's. "But it is, isn't it?"

Rayanne couldn't do anything but smile sadly, like an apology. Carina pressed closer to her and Rayanne let her take one of her hands gingerly.

"It's okay," Carina whispered, and Rayanne sniffled. She refused to acknowledge the tears running down her face by wiping at them. Instead, she just burrowed closer to her sister, trying to soak in the warmth she felt coming from Carina's body.

chapter thirteen

AS SHE EXPECTED, Rayanne immediately hated the hospital. Half of the nurses were overly friendly and touchy-feely, and the rest were curt and impatient. The art on the walls was generic and ugly. The air was stale and suffocating. The food was fatty and tasteless. And then there was the overlying sense of incarceration, because she knew she couldn't leave even if she wanted to.

Rayanne loathed every inch of it.

When she saw Dr. Biri, so familiar and reassuring, Ray nearly threw her arms around her.

While in inpatient, Rayanne was referred and connected with other services, such as a nutritionist, a psychiatrist, a counsellor and a support group. Dr. Biri called this collection of people her "team", and Rayanne's "work" with her team would begin immediately.

Apparently, winding up in the ER meant being bumped to the top of any mental health wait list.

Cal and Hannah visited numerous times a day, which was just about the most awkward, depressing part of it all. Hannah pretended she didn't want to cry and Rayanne pretended that she didn't realize this; Cal was usually the one talking, giving Rayanne updates on the plants in the sunroom. He even visited Forever Home on her behalf, and showed her the blurry snapshots of excited dogs that he took on his phone.

Rayanne had told her sisters not to come often, since she wouldn't be in the hospital for long and hated being seen in this way. But her sisters texted constantly, and so did Charmayne and Madison.

Rayanne was nervous talking to her friends. Embarrassed, because of where she was calling them from. But nonetheless, they sounded happy to hear her voice. They asked how it was going, and Rayanne told them it was okay, but that she wanted to come home.

Charmayne disclosed, in her intuitive off-hand way, that Josh was asking about her.

Rayanne scrolled through her and Josh's Facebook messages, reading old snippets of conversations where all they talked about were movies and music.

He didn't message her, and Rayanne didn't know exactly what to say. So she settled on a simple, one-line message: *Hear any good tunes lately?*

The next day, Rayanne got her first item in the hospital's daily mail run – Josh's old iPod, scratched and covered in stickers, but packed with thousands of songs.

THEY SAID THAT RAYANNE needed to make better coping mechanisms, but she didn't know how. She could see the logic in each doctor and nurse's eyes: how the so-called "solution" was so simple for them, all laid-out in the neat format of doctors' studies and the DSM-5. But their logic didn't translate to Rayanne. She went through their motions but nothing inside her felt relieved, only subdued.

She started to pretend that she didn't have a body at all.

She spent every morning showering and changing her clothes, with her eyes squeezed firmly shut.

She didn't dare look at herself. It was bad enough that she could feel the newly acquired fat and insulation beginning to sit on her bones; she didn't want to see it. She refused to see it.

Rayanne had been under the illusion that gaining weight back would be easier when she was emaciated. Because then, she might be able to convince herself that she actually did need it. If she was in a hospital, if enough people told her to eat, if she could feel each of her ribs, then surely she could let herself gain a few pounds.

In the end, though, it didn't matter. Gaining was gaining.

After everything, the only real thing Rayanne felt was exhaustion. She was too tired in her mind and in her body, too exhausted to fight the demons inside of her or the people who tried to help her do it.

So she stopped trying to fight, and instead she did anything and everything they asked her to.

There was nothing strong or heroic about this. Rayanne didn't feel any sort of relief or exhilaration in the letting go.

Instead, she felt the absolute life-draining shame of giving up.

Rayanne told the truth in therapy, but without feeling and without inflection, like it was not her truth but someone else's.

Her bones began to disappear and colour came back to her cheeks. She might not have been getting worse, but she didn't feel better. She didn't know what would make her feel better.

It was in this state that Rayanne was let back out into the world.

chapter fourteen

RAYANNE SWORE THAT her house smelled better on Christmas day. It was sweet, somehow, and warmer in a different way than on August afternoons. Logically, it probably had to do with the waffles Hannah made for breakfast, and the spices Cal put in the eggnog that Jordie always drank too much of.

That year, Ray was more aware of these things than before. The house's vibrant walls, saturated with paint and years-old Christmas decorations, were a welcome contrast from the hospital's. She'd only left two weeks ago, and sounds were often too loud.

Hannah made Christmas breakfast while listening to music. It's one of the only times Rayanne would ever see her mother throw herself into a meal. Hannah didn't exactly have patience for cooking: in her words it was messy, time-consuming, and unpredictable. She made an exception for Christmas morning.

Technically, the Ukrainian Orthodox Christmas takes place in January. But her family celebrated on the 25th of December anyway, mostly because it was easier that way. They still had a traditional Christmas dinner at Hannah's mother's every January.

Rayanne stood uncertainly near the kitchen counters. The waffle iron beeped, signalling it was ready, but the sound was nearly drowned out by Stevie Wonder's voice crooning about a Christmas tree. Hannah stood ready with a cupful of batter, and though she hadn't cooked a single waffle, Rayanne could already smell them.

Her stomach rumbled, still dragging itself out of *starvation mode* despite the weight gain.

Amy moved past Hannah, holding an empty bacon package, her nose wrinkled, before throwing it in the trash. Jordie hip-checked her away in order to get into the cutlery drawer. Carina poured orange juice into a jug with ice cubes, while Cal pulled a bottle of champagne from the fridge.

Out in the back yard, Echo barked at crows as she ran through the snow.

Behind Rayanne's shoulder, Edie rattled on incessantly. *An entire waffle is probably 240 calories and maple syrup would add another 100 and that fruit salad would be around 150 because fruit has sugar and the orange juice is 120 and who knows how many calories are in champagne we've never even had champagne oh my god how many does that add up to like over 600 which is more than we should eat in like a day oh my god —*

Edie was talking faster, because she was getting used to Rayanne cutting her off now. But though Rayanne managed to shut her up occasionally, it never took away from having heard her in the first place. Rayanne couldn't just *un-know* those numbers, and the only thing she could manage at this point was attempting to flat-out ignore them.

As Rayanne watched her family make Christmas breakfast, she tried to feel the music and laugh when Cal struggled to open the champagne bottle without breaking a window. But ignoring Edie took up most of her attention.

Sitting down to breakfast twenty minutes later, she forced a smile when she clinked glasses with her family. As they ate, each bite for Rayanne was a conscious effort to slam the door shut on the voice crowding her head. As she felt the food sitting heavily in her stomach, and wished with all her might she could throw it up, she forced herself to swallow around her panic. She hoped tomorrow, or the day after that, she would start to win her battle.

Rayanne hadn't had the chance to shop for presents herself, so instead her presents were items picked out by Hannah (except for Hannah's, which were picked out by Cal). The experience felt dishonest and wrong.

Rayanne organized her own presents into a humble pile on the couch – a *Dazed and Confused* t-shirt, a book about digital filmmaking, a card symbolizing a kennel sponsorship at Forever Home, and a collection of gift cards.

Cal had sprung and bought Ray a pair of headphones that she knew were too expensive. It was why she hadn't even technically asked for them, just watched the commercials with envy and pursed lips. Her dad must have noticed.

"They're noise-cancelling," Cal explained, sitting on the couch beside Ray as she attempted to free the headphones from their plastic vice-grip packaging. "So your sisters' voices won't be a backtrack anymore."

Ray smiled, the cautious kind. All of her smiles were,

these days; almost as if she wasn't convinced it was allowed. A part of her demanded she be demure because it felt like penance. She was ingrained with guilt over what she'd put her family through: guilt for starting it in the first place, and guilt for not speaking up sooner.

By this time a few different professionals had told her it wasn't her fault. But she still felt fault in every line of her body.

When paramedics crouched beside a victim they always repeated *it's going to be okay*, because that's what they were trained to do and say. To Ray this was no different. The psychiatrist, therapist and nutritionist were all reciting the line *it's not your fault*, but at the end of the day it didn't stick because they didn't know Rayanne; they hadn't seen what happened, but were only assembling the pieces.

Rayanne sat thick in the memories of what she had done, when there was never anyone else around. It was always her own hands that hurt her. So whose fault was it?

Guilt was uncomfortable. It was almost as uncomfortable as the weight of Christmas breakfast, poking idly at Ray's stomach as she sat beside her dad.

The headphones finally sprung from the plastic, she worked to undo the twist tie around the chord.

"Have you seen my iPod?" she asked, glancing at the coffee table. Ever since inpatient, she hardly went anywhere without it. She'd started using music as a coping mechanism when she was in hospital. Along with Josh's music, the iPod now held her favourites: Peter Tosh, Jack Johnson, Al Green, Jefferson Airplane and Bob Marley.

Cal reached for the side table and passed her the iPod. Rayanne plugged the headphone jack into the device, feeling the satisfying *click* run through her fingers.

She'd already had one outrageously large meal and

knew it wouldn't be long before Cal was preparing a second. Her stocking was filled with chocolates she wasn't certain she would eat and overriding all of this was the glaring knowledge that she used to love this day and it used to be easy, but it wasn't anymore.

She used to soothe herself by insisting *I can stop whenever I want to*, but she found her hands shaking. She would give anything to turn this thing off, to have her eating disorder erased from her mind for twenty-four hours, so she could have Christmas day to just *eat*. The most simple, human thing.

But she couldn't, not for this day or even long enough to have breakfast in peace.

Rayanne always thought that she would decide to recover exactly once. That she would reach a point where circumstances – always unnamed, always half-imagined – would cause her to throw her hands up and say *I quit, please help me, I can't do this anymore*. And in a way, that's what had happened. What nobody had told her, was that recovery would turn out to be that moment repeating itself over and over. It was relentless.

Pushing down anxiety, Rayanne put the headphones over her ears. And everything went quiet.

Carina and Jordie's bubbly voices were muffled; the Roger Whittaker song coming from the kitchen was silenced completely. Rayanne smiled, easier this time, and scrolled to her favourite Bob Marley song.

The steel drums pulsed against the drums of her ears. Rayanne relaxed into the couch, feeling her sleeve brush against her dad's. He was reading the book Hannah had bought him: something non-fiction about true crime and motorcycle gangs.

Carina and Jordie sat cross-legged on the living room

floor, in front of the tree. Wrapping paper still surrounded them, like the ending scene in *A Christmas Story*. Carina had asked for, and received, a DIY kit for friendship bracelets. She tied a pink and purple one around Jordie's wrist.

Through the kitchen doorway, Rayanne could see Amy sitting at the kitchen table. She gestured animatedly as she talked to Hannah, who stood at the kitchen counter, wrapping up the remnants of their breakfast. Echo sat dutifully at Hannah's feet, warm brown eyes keen on the possibility of food.

When Amy wasn't looking, Hannah slipped the dog a piece of leftover waffle.

Somehow, with the absence of noise but the overlay of music, things became clearer. Rayanne focused on the solid warmth of her father beside her and the way Carina and Jordie's eyes found each other's when they were talking. The love she felt in her heart when she looked at them *hurt*. It never had before.

The door to the sunroom stood open, and afternoon light spilled over the carpet. The winter sun could be blinding in the prairies, and Rayanne knew that patch of carpet was warm as summer. As a kid, she'd lie and daydream for hours. No music required, just the ambient sounds of her parents puttering in the house and the birds twittering on the other side of the glass.

Rayanne made it her silent goal to be able to daydream in that room again.

It was dark outside by the time Cal started making Christmas supper. Amy, Jordie, and Carina picked up the same routine as that morning. Hannah was camped out on the couch with a glass of wine and a new e-reader.

Rayanne perched at the kitchen doorway.

"I get dibs on making stuffing!" Jordie shouted, ducking into a cupboard. Carina gave a snort.

"Go for it." she said, braiding the bread dough she'd prepared that afternoon, "It comes from a box and is, hands-down, the easiest thing to make."

"No need to get competitive," Jordie teased. "It's just cooking, Martha Stewart."

Amy laughed as she washed potatoes in the sink. "Pot and kettle, man."

Jordie gave her a light punch on the shoulder.

"Hey, behave, you two." Cal bent in front of the oven. He motioned to the girls to back away. "And watch it – I'm opening this to check on the bird."

Carina and Jordie moved away dutifully.

"Poor birdie," Amy muttered. "Dead birdie."

"Okay." Jordie rolled her eyes. "Somebody get the vegan out of the kitchen."

Rayanne felt her lip tug in a smile, almost a laugh. Cal straightened and closed the oven door. Amy returned to the potatoes in the sink and Carina started on her bread again, Jordie picked up the box of stuffing and read the back.

"Do you ever notice how, when Donald Duck celebrates Christmas, he still cooks turkey?" Amy demanded of the room at large. "How messed up is that? He's a *duck*."

Carina and Amy exchanged a look. Cal stood with a shocked expression.

"That *is* messed up," he said, and Carina and Jordie laughed.

Suddenly, Rayanne was filled with the sensation of being on the outside of something, looking in. Like she was only on the fringes of this family, this life, this day, without ever being *in* it.

Shaken, she took a step forward into the light and warmth of the kitchen. Amy looked up from the sink. "Oh, hey – wanna set the table?" she asked.

Rayanne swallowed and looked at the kitchen table, where their Christmas china sat waiting. Setting the table had been Rayanne's preferred chore for years, only now her family knew why: it kept her away from the food.

"Actually," Rayanne said, turning back to Amy, "can I help?" She nodded tentatively toward the kitchen.

Amy just stared at her. Jordie put the box of stuffing down slowly, glancing at Carina, whose hands were frozen above a loaf tin as she looked at Rayanne with a blank expression. Cal blinked.

Then Amy smiled and said, "Yeah, of course. Here – you take over the potatoes. I have to make the perogie dough."

Amy brought her hands from the sink water. Jordie and Carina relaxed, and Cal just watched as Rayanne walked to the sink and began scrubbing potatoes.

Within seconds, the banter from before picked up again. Rayanne washed and peeled and boiled the potatoes, moving around her sisters and dad within the confines of their tiny kitchen. With each step, Rayanne could actually feel her feet touching ground.

She'd outright believed that she would have to redeem and change herself in order to be loveable again. To be *enough*. But right then, just the simple act of being there in that moment with them, felt like enough. So maybe she was enough; maybe she always had been.

chapter fifteen

WHILE SITTING IN THE SUNROOM, it occurred to Rayanne that the feeling of warm wind on her skin was one of her favourite things. She wrote it down in her journal. This one was the colour of a soft blue and had an ornately drawn tree on the front.

It was a cold night in December when Carrie and Ray had burned the old one.

This one held song lyrics, haikus and doodles. Mostly, though, it held long-winded entries of Rayanne's own words. And that morning, just hours before her graduation ceremony, she knew she had to let her stage-induced anxiety out onto the page.

In a few hours I'll be walking across a stage downtown and my hands will be clasped around a diploma instead of this journal. Until then I'm tucked away in my sunroom. The windows are open to the

June morning and I can smell the flowers blooming outside.

There are many things about this past year that I don't like to remember. Things like hiding from people, to the point that they became strangers. I don't like to think about how cold I was. Or the feeling of waking up in a hospital.

I can't hide or run from these memories. And the worst thing about them is that, even though I know they give me nightmares, on bad days I still wish I could go back. I didn't put myself through pain and starvation for no reason at all. The hard truth is, for very complex reasons, Edie gave me comfort.

I used to hate myself for that. There was a long period of time when the only thing I could manage to do was blame myself for every single disordered thing I did. I had to learn to let it go.

Feel the itch of wanting to scrape myself down to the bone.

Let it go.

Shake with the need to tally every number.

Let it go.

Recognize the absolute necessity to assume the identity of a "skinny" person.

Close my eyes. Take a breath.

Then Let It Go.

Sometimes it's a day at a time. Sometimes, it's by the hours. And on some days I have to white knuckle each breath.

Many people think that because I'm a "normal" weight, that I am recovered. And that's okay. I understand now that no one besides me will ever know what it is I am experiencing. But this won't stop me from asking for help when I need it. Even if I have to chant to myself – it's okay to ask for help.

It's okay to ask for help.

It's okay to ask for help.

Until I believe it.

I can't help but think about the other terrible things that may have happened to my classmates since our freshman year. Maybe their parents got divorced, or their grandmother got cancer. Maybe they lost a sibling to drugs or violence, maybe they started cutting themselves, maybe they got pregnant.

I know that we all have a lot more troubles than we really should have, so it's not surprising if along the way we get lost and turn to the wrong things to make us feel better. Sometimes, it's nobody's fault.

Josh and I are going to graduation together. And I'm so nervous, but nerves can be good because they mean I'm trying something new. There is so much in life that is supposed to take up your time, your energy, and your heart. I had to learn that all over again. It was like re-teaching myself how to walk or write. I had to learn how to sit still and watch a movie, how to have fun with friends, how to sleep in, how to eat at restaurants. How to eat, period.

I struggled for a long time with what to call myself. So many different words: anorexic, bulimic, disordered, recovered, relapsed, recovering, curvy, fat, thin, pretty, plain, ugly, normal.

Labels never work, no matter which way you try to spin it.

The only word that seems right is my name. It embraces every beauty mark; allows for each imperfection.

"Rayanne."

The name used to feel awkward on my tongue. Now, it sounds like something finally shifting into place.

Rayanne closed her journal. Beside her, the mandevillas she planted back in the fall reached up for the dusty panes of glass. The temperature was even warmer than outside: probably 27 degrees. The carpet below her was warm, the sun so bright on her skin.

Rayanne pressed her arm to her nose. She kept her eyes open, taking in the tiny, white-blond hair covering her skin. It moved every time her breath pushed out of her nose.

When she breathed in, she didn't smell soap or the body spray she'd stolen from Carina. She just smelled like *her* – like the indescribable scent of her skin and how heavy she'd slept on her sheets the night before. She closed her eyes, and as she breathed in again, Rayanne thought about how once upon a time, she'd been born into this world as someone who'd loved herself.

Taking a breath, Rayanne lay back on the carpet. She set her journal down a little ways from her, and then folded her hands on top of her stomach. It was softer now.

A distant, cold voice called to her. And Rayanne smiled, knowing that she didn't have to answer at all. That she didn't have to do anything but lie there and soak in the rays of sunlight she'd spent so long missing.

Closing her eyes, Rayanne sighed and let herself daydream.

Acknowledgements

Many bright lights and kindred spirits have had their hands in keeping this story afloat. I love you all.

My most humble and heartfelt thanks goes out to: Lynn Corbett, who saw perseverance in me when I felt most weak. My editor, Kathy Stinson, whose endless patience and wisdom was so very much needed. Trixie Hennessey, for helping me re-discover puddles.

Shane Koyczan, Dallas Green and Justin Furstenfeld, whose creative voices taught me how to find my own, and who will forever be the music behind this story.

My teachers at VFS, for validating and nurturing a girl's obsession with fiction. Terry Erickson, who took me seriously in a world where I never felt heard. Jessica Latimer, Ana Ono and Silla Leudottir, whose friendship and love changed who I am.

My most desperate thanks go to my family – my grandparents Gerry and Gail, who gave me a safe space to create and grow. Auntie Lesley, for always making me feel loved and important. All of my amazing cousins, who made my childhood better than a kid could hope for. My little sister Teagan, who taught me to find the strength I didn't know I had. Solanos, Daisy and Castiel, who are the four-legged lights of my life. And Molly, who was the sliver of sunlight in my darkest times – I miss you every day.

This whole book is already dedicated to them, but I still have to thank my parents, Godfrey and Darcey. You two truly are my heroes.

About the Author

Small Displays of Chaos is the first novel from emerging writer Breanna Fischer, and is based on her own experience being diagnosed as anorexic with bulimic behaviors in 2010.

Though constantly creating stories since the age of seven, Bre didn't seriously consider writing until she was twenty-two years old and halfway through a University degree for Studio Art. Extremely unhappy with her studies, Bre dropped everything to chase down the conviction that she was a writer.

In 2014, Bre was accepted into the Writing For Film & Television program at Vancouver Film School, where she studied writing for features, teleplay, sketches, comic books, and animation. Her short script, inspired by a single moment of *Small Displays of Chaos*, was produced and made into a short film in 2015.

Known for coming-of-age dramas and offbeat comedy, Bre is a versatile writer whose skills span from poetry to feature films. She now resides in Vancouver, British Columbia, where she plans to stay indefinitely.

Printed by Imprimerie Gauvin
Gatineau, Québec